Shipwreck
at
Sleeping Bear

By
Robin Shutt

Llumina Press

ISBN: 1-932560-75-0
Printed in the United States of America by Llumina Press

DEDICATION

Shipwreck at Sleeping Bear would not have been imagined or written without the encouragement and love of Lynne Sandra, who inspired me to explore the creativity within me. My passion for this magical region would never have been ignited if not for Gratia Lucy, who shared with me the wonderful warm embrace found in the waters that fill the Great Lakes. An appreciation for all things spiritual would never have been formed without Anne Elizabeth, who helped me discover the hope and harmony inherent in Native American culture. Many of the adventures fictionalized in this work would never have been experienced without the opportunity to live, work and play in the pleasant peninsula that is Michigan. And so I dedicate this to everyone and everything in my life that has made this possible.

Acknowledgements

Shipwreck at Sleeping Bear is a story that relates in large part to the experiences I had while growing up in Michigan. To add substance to my experience I referenced bits and pieces of the following books: *The History of the Ottawa and Chippewa Indians of Michigan* by Chief A.J. Blackbird; *Mysteries and Histories: Shipwrecks on the Great Lakes* by W. Oleszeski; *Great Lakes Shipwrecks and Survivals* by W. Ratigan; *Michigan's Lumbertowns* by J.W. Kilpan; *The Ojibwa* by H.H. Tanman; *Ojibway Heritage* by B. Johnson. I am indebted to the authors for their good work. I am also grateful for the wonderful work of my editor, Leslie Clearwater. Her clear eye and strong vision made this work better than I imagined it could be.

PROLOGUE

Sometimes people change their world without even trying. This is a story about one such serendipitous change. It involves three young adults who were simply living: no activism, no hidden agendas. They were too busy enjoying life as best they knew how.

One youth came from wealth, another from a working-class family, and the third from an ancient village hidden deep in the forest. Each was following a clear path to adulthood on a trail their ancestors had blazed for them. No one questioned his or her direction. No one, that is, until one fateful summer when the trio helped two very different civilizations learn to live together.

The geographical distance separating the two civilizations was slight, just as the cultural gap between them was vast. Native Americans had lived in the northwest corner of Michigan's Lower Peninsula for more than three hundred and fifty years; they called their homeland Tawkenin. Those of European descent had moved into the region less than one hundred years ago and lived twenty miles south of Tawkenin, in a village named Harbor Springs. The two cultures co-existed reasonably well, mostly by staying out of each other's way, until one particular summer at the mid-point of the twentieth century.

These three young adults will now relate the events of that summer as they remember them. They do so in the hope that you will understand how the values embraced by society mirror the ideals of its people, and vice versa.

Chapter One

New Moon

Saturday, May 27

AUPETCHI

My name is Aupetchi and I am Native American. During the summer we speak of, which was long ago, the *waubesh*, or white people, just called us "Indian." That's when they were being kind. I was seventeen then and didn't know where they got that term. I thought they had just made a mistake. We called ourselves the Anabe, which means the people, and I thought "Indian" was their way of saying Anabe. I have since learned that this is not so. I am glad I did not know it then.

My involvement really began during my thirteenth summer, when my vision quest revealed my destiny. Every Anabe boy went on a vision quest to find his purpose in life, marking his passage from boy to man. During my quest I learned that my destiny would mirror that of my father, my grandfather, my grandfather's father, and my grandfather's grandfather: I was to serve as Odawgen, the messenger, as had they. Odawgen filled a revered and honorable ceremonial role for the Anabe, so this destiny pleased me.

Now, four years later, I was preparing to serve my people once again. Every year, on the morning after the first new moon following the final snowfall of winter, Odawgen emerged. I can remember that morning as clearly as if it were yesterday.

I woke before dawn and crawled out of my *wigwom*, stretching. Since I was about to enter Michi Gama, the monster lake, I had to prepare myself according to tradition. I secured an ornamental pouch crafted from the stomach of a moose around my waist. Then I bowed reverently to the four directions and thanked Manitou, the Great Spirit, for selecting me to perform the sacred ritual I was about to begin.

I was the tallest man in the village, although my height had never been formally measured. This was not the way of the Anabe. We saw no reason to quantify the obvious. With dark brown eyes I looked through tousled strands of hair and concentrated upon a distant vision only I could see, silently centering myself. Walking to the lakeshore I reached down and cupped a handful of clean cool water. I drizzled the cleansing water over my body and smeared my skin with bear fat to protect me from the icy water. Then I stepped into the lake's shallow rim ready to begin my ceremonial swim. A small and eager crowd had gathered to see me off in the dim light of dawn.

There were two major villages in Tawkenin, our homeland, separated by a thick coniferous forest. During the short dry season at the end of the summer, travel between them was easy. However during the long wet season, the middle of which we were now in, it was not. Consequently, what would have been be a half-day stroll on dry land was now a two-day journey through a cold, soggy marsh.

Fortunately a small bay bordered both villages and provided quick travel during the wet seasons. Normally we used canoes, but not on this day of celebration. On this day Odawgen swam the bay from the south village to the north village, carrying the waterproof pouch that held the first communication with the outside world - the *waubesh* world - since the initial frost of winter. Odawgen's arrival in the north village, the larger of the two, started a ten-day celebration called *Memegot*, or the Reading of the Good News. *Memegot* commemorated our peaceful solution to European settlement.

When Europeans first appeared on our shores, we welcomed them. They told us that they only wanted to trade with us. They said that they would never settle on our land. They lied. Years later, and after numerous skirmishes, they still remained. They even built a wooden village of their own, south of Tawkenin.

When it became clear that they would never leave we

decided to approach them to negotiate a permanent peace. We sent a small band of revered elders through the wet spring marsh to speak with the *waubesh* leaders. Our message was simple: You are welcome to stay in the wooden village you have built upon our land, but leave our sacred homeland and peaceful villages alone.

We hoped that the *waubesh* would see the wisdom of compromise and quickly agree to avoid further bloodshed. They delayed their decision for weeks. They eventually agreed to our terms, but at the last possible moment.

Expecting the worst, we had secretly assembled a large band of warriors in the north village. They were instructed to attack if word of *waubesh* acceptance did not reach them by sunset. Our elders became unnerved, knowing that there was not enough time to walk the news of agreement back to the north village. They would be able to reach the nearer south village by early afternoon, but the swamp separating the two villages blocked further passage: They wouldn't get to the north village until the following morning, too late to stop the violence they had planned.

Furthermore, the entire fleet of Anabe canoes was in the north village at the disposal of the anxious warriors, eliminating the option of traveling upon the rapidly thawing bay. The *waubesh* offered no relief, refusing to trust us with their boats. They said it was our problem. We knew that if we did attack they would never again consider compromise.

So with all alternatives exhausted the elders decided that the youngest and strongest of the group should make the journey alone. He would run to the south village, then swim the final leg to the north. He would race the sunset, hoping to reach the anxious warriors in time. The young man's name was Aushegun.

Against all odds Aushegun made the journey in time, nearly freezing as he swam the final arduous leg. He immediately went to see Sawnish, the most revered Anabe wise man, and the only Anabe who could read the written agreement the *waubesh* had drafted. He read the good news to the nervous warriors just before the sun set. Aushegun prevented an unnecessary war and ushered in the peace that had been preserved ever since.

My swim would open this year's celebration, so the appreciative throng gathered around me whooped approvingly as I walked further into the water. When it reached above my knees I dove in and began to swim. Although few knew it, my stroke mimicked Aushegun's. My feet were completely submerged, giving me a strong kick. My head and shoulders were extended out of the water as I pulled myself forward.

Sawnish's descendant Sawmay lived in the north village and held the same seat of honor first obtained by his ancestor. Tradition dictated that Sawmay would read the first written words of this spring – words that I carried. I moved through the water easily, leaving the people and the south village behind me. The crowd's roar diminished, then vanished from my ears. I was alone in the water. Although I did not know it, the fate of my people was sealed in my waterproof pouch.

KATE

My name is Kate Kilpatrick and I was also 17 years old that summer. I wouldn't turn 18 until the fall, but I was already nervous about it. My mother had told me that that's when I would become a woman. I couldn't imagine how that could be since I usually felt closer to 12 than 20, at least mentally. I thought of myself as a young girl. I loved to play in the water and run on the beach and do silly girl things. I read Nancy Drew novels and imagined myself in all sorts of wild adventures. I enjoyed being a child and was in no hurry to grow up.

But when I looked in a mirror, I didn't see a young girl. The fact that I saw a woman scared me. The men who frequented the restaurant where I worked made it worse. It was clear that they thought I looked like a woman, and a desirable one at that. This did please me to a certain extent: I wanted to be attractive. Mostly, though, I was embarrassed by it. What were these old men doing gawking at a girl like me? Didn't they have wives or girlfriends?

I was tall then, about 5' 9", taller than I am now. My mother always told me I had a well-proportioned body, although I thought she was just being well, motherly. When I looked in the mirror all I saw was a big butt and small boobs. I wasn't comfortable with my body at all.

My face was another story. I loved my sea-green eyes and my small, perfectly formed nose. My eyebrows were thin and my eyelashes were naturally long and silky. I had a long face with even, subtle cheekbones. My lips were full, but not too full. People constantly complimented my face. When I was young they called me "pretty," "cute," "button," things like that. Not just friends of the family either, but strangers in the street and even my brothers, which is what convinced me it was true. My brothers were merciless when it came to teasing me, but they never made fun of my face.

So mom was right, I was becoming a woman. And in some ways I even acted like one. I had a boyfriend. His name was Cole Harrison and I felt so lucky that he noticed me and genuinely liked me. He made me feel grown up.

This was the start of our third summer together. We still did a lot of childish things, like wrestling and having water fights. But it was when we were alone that I knew I was a woman. My body reacted to his presence in wonderful ways; reactions that I knew could not come from a girl. But when he was away from me I felt like a youngster again: confused about life, anxious about the future, and certain that I was the most unattractive, miserable girl on Earth (albeit, with a pretty face). In a word, I was confused.

I lived in the small town of Harbor Springs, on a part of Lake Michigan called Little Traverse Bay. My mother managed a restaurant where I worked during the summer. I went to high school in the winter. I had just finished my junior year.

Not many people lived up there back then, at least not year round. If you counted all the neighboring towns and villages you might get to five thousand, five thousand white people, that is. It was obvious that white Europeans had settled the area. We did have Native Americans too. They lived north of town. For some reason we did not include them in our census.

We called the remote woods where they lived L'Arbre Croche, French for Crooked Tree. The French were the first to name it so their term lingered on, although most people I knew used the English version. It was a good name since a large crooked pine tree dominated its shoreline. The pine served as a navigational guide to the sailors traveling on Lake Michigan, just as it had to the voyageurs, warriors and explorers who came before them.

The Native Americans called themselves the Anabe, which I knew because my best friend was one. Her name was May and she was one of the few Anabe who went to our school.

◆◆◆

This day had started for me with a visit to Robin's Ice Cream Parlor, home of Harbor Springs best homemade ice cream. Only locals knew about it. It was on the corner of Ann Street and West Bluff, too far from the harbor for the tourists to find, which was good because more and more tourists visited us each summer. We needed a place where we could escape and for me, Robin's was it.

I went in, placed my order, and scanned the posters tacked to the wall. One in particular caught my eye. I directed my comment to the freckle-faced girl scooping raspberry ice cream into my sugar cone. "Labor Day sounds like a gas."

"How's that?" the girl replied, digging deep into the floor model freezer to the bottom of a nearly empty three-gallon tub.

"Labor Day. You know, the Harbor Festival," I clarified.

The festival was a Harbor Springs tradition to celebrate the end of the summer. It featured boat races, crop competitions, bake-offs, livestock judging, and carnival rides. The crowd that gathered for it was as eclectic as Emmet County itself, which ran north and east from Harbor Springs, through the dense forest that camouflaged the Anabe homeland, to the Straits of Mackinac.

"That's too far away for me to worry about," said the server. "Fifty-three cents please." She handed me the cone so I thanked her, gave her seventy-five cents and exited the parlor. I walked slowly down West Bluff enjoying the view of Lake Michigan and Little Traverse Bay as I ate my cone. It was a beautiful, cloudless day: a perfect way to start the summer season.

After descending the bluff I turned onto State Street and joined a large crowd moving down the sidewalk. A few pedestrians window-shopped at the stores lining the way. Some moved purposefully towards the crowded pier on the west end of town. Many - too many in my eyes -

ducked into the numerous "famous" Mackinac fudge shops that had curiously materialized in many northern Michigan towns.

Almost everyone was from down south: Lower Michigan, Indiana, Illinois, or Ohio. They had flocked up north for the Memorial Day Weekend, the first of the summer season. We called them fudgies, mocking their love for the sweet. Despite this sarcastic term we did not find their excursion into town invasive, at least not yet.

I ducked out of the main current and turned down onto Main Street, cut across Zorn Park and headed towards the White Pine Inn where I worked. This would be my fifth summer working for my mother in the restaurant there. I slowed down as I neared the inn, enjoying the warmth of the bright morning sun on my face. Climbing the loading dock that led into the kitchen, I hoped that Cole would call me soon. I couldn't wait to tell him about the newest addition to the Harbor Festival.

COLE

I can still see her ascending the loading dock to enter the kitchen. I was about 100 yards away, on the deck of the White Pine swimming pool, preparing for my morning workout. I always started after she arrived, just so I could watch her walk up those stairs.

After Kate entered the kitchen I would climb into the shallow end of the pool and temper my body by falling backwards into the heated, chlorinated water. This was Harbor Springs only rectangular in-ground pool. I used it five days a week. My family had summered in Harbor Springs for more than fifty years and was a generous community benefactor, and so the White Pine let me train in their "guests only" pool.

I was 18 years old, six feet tall and weighed 180 pounds. I had been lifting weights for three years so I had broad shoulders, well-developed arms, a muscular torso and strong, sinuous legs. My prep school coach told me I had a classic swimmer's body: lean, powerful, and fluid.

I had thick black hair that I cut often, and fast-growing whiskers that I shaved relentlessly from my face and neck. I couldn't believe how hairy I was. I had to shave my legs, arms, chest, and stomach before my biggest races. Fortunately and much to the satisfaction of both Kate and myself my back was hairless.

Kate told me I was handsome, but I think she was just being nice. I have a conspicuous protruding forehead, a result of my mother's Welsh roots, and deep-set hazel eyes. My teammates in prep school called me the "Missing Link" because of my simian features. I know they meant it as a joke, but it still hurt, even though Kate said I had a good sense of humor.

My permanent home was just outside Detroit, in an exclusive suburb called Birmingham. My parents believed that the more exclusive something was, the better. I didn't really care because I was away at school most of the time anyway, except during the summer, when we came up here. Our summer "cottage," as they called it, was in a gated community west of Harbor Springs called Harbor Point.

We spent all summer there: my father, mother, sister and an entourage that included a butler, two valets, two housekeepers, a chauffeur, gardener, cook and boatman. My parents did not travel light. All but the gardener and boatman worked for us year-round. At the Point we were surrounded by some of the Midwest's wealthiest families, with the poorest checking in with a net worth of least $20 million. We were not one of the poorest.

The wealth that surrounded me disinterested me and I felt detached from the world my parents had built. I didn't know how I wanted to live, but I knew that I didn't want to turn out like them. Nothing much appealed to me but nothing much bored me, especially when summering at the Point. I was what you'd call indifferent. I'd take in a party now and then, and when Kate was working, some friends and I would head out on the family Chris Craft cruiser, the *Lumber Baron*. It was a beautiful vessel, made out of mahogany and well appointed. It had a raised pilothouse, or bridge, and two overnight cabins. Nothing but the best, remember. We'd have the boatman motor us down Lake Michigan to Charlevoix or up north to Mackinac.

Only two things interested me. One was Kate. She was nothing like my parents, and knew nothing of their world, which was perfect. With her I could do things my parents would never dream of, like go to Juilleret's for dinner and ice cream.

My other passion was competitive swimming. I started competing at age six and blossomed at fifteen. The past spring I had accepted a full scholarship to swim at Michigan State College in East Lansing. My father wanted me to go to an Ivy League school, but I knew they'd only be interested in my athletic ability and the family money, not my brain. I hoped it would be different at State.

So this was going to be my final summer at the Point. I would dedicate the next four years, summers included, to my collegiate swimming career. The only snag in this plan was Kate. I had fallen in love with her. I didn't know where our relationship was going, but I knew I didn't want to lose her.

I also didn't know that my father had a loftier goal for me, as usual. He had mentioned it once a while back, and I brushed it off because it was so absurd. It never crossed my mind again, until this summer. His plan was for me to train for, and win, an Olympic Gold Medal.

Chapter Two

WAXING QUARTER

Saturday, June 3

COLE

I suppose I should tell you how my family got rich. Most people are curious about that. Fortunately, my father had a book published about it, with pictures and everything. He says it's to preserve our family history. Anyway, you're probably interested too, so here goes.

In August of 1833, my great-great-grandfather, Winston Harrison, married Cassandra Fraser in London, England. There's a copy of their wedding portrait in father's book and I remember thinking how pretty she was, even when I was small boy. She had dark hair, porcelain skin and penetrating eyes. Anyway, at Winston and Cassandra's wedding reception her first cousin, James Fraser, persuaded Winston to relocate with him to the United States. James promised Winston unimagined riches if he helped settle a marshy area at the mouth of a broad, shallow river in the distant Michigan Territory. Winston agreed and the two men left London the following spring, leaving Cassandra behind. This always bothered me. Why get married if you were going to leave your wife, especially one as beautiful as she?

Anyway, they crossed the ocean without incident and started to clear the area. The Indians were kind enough, meaning they didn't kill them. I suspect this was because they had little interest in the swampy, mosquito-infested watershed the duo claimed as their own. Fraser couldn't pronounce the word the Indians used to describe the region, but he tried and ended up naming the river the "Saginaw."

The first year was pretty rough, but the pair gutted it out and their diligence was rewarded. The following spring a few hearty souls joined them and a small settlement started to grow, which they named Lower Saginaw. The next spring Cassandra joined them, finally. She was not impressed. Lower Saginaw was clearly not London. The only saving grace was that James Fraser kept his promise to Winston. Both men were getting rich.

The following January, Michigan became the 26th State of the Union. James and Winston's Saginaw Bay Company flourished more than ever, as did their settlement, which they renamed Bay City. Four years later Cassandra delivered a daughter, Anne. Six years after this Winston dissolved his partnership with Fraser, becoming sole owner of half of Bay City's thriving lumber mills. Winston Harrison was now rich.

In 1858, Winston befriended a visiting New Yorker named Henry Sage. He introduced Sage to his daughter Anne, now a teenager, and the two fell in love. In 1859 Cassandra died after delivering Winston Harrison the Second. One year later Anne married Henry Sage, whom Winston took on as partner. The War Between the States created great demand for Michigan lumber, so ten years later, Henry Sage joined Winston as one of the wealthiest men in the now affluent Saginaw River valley.

In 1871, Sage liquidated the partnership and moved back to New York City, taking Anne with him. This left only the widowed Winston and his young son, whom he called Two, to run the business. Unfortunately, Two had little interest in business. He spent the next two decades chasing whores, gambling, having a brief marriage, and fathering Winston Three. Winston the First continued to run the sawmills until the entire river valley, including her many tributaries, was stripped of its prized native white pine. It took less than forty years.

All the available lumber had been harvested, milled and shipped east. All that was left was the barren marsh that had first greeted Winston the First and James Fraser. When Winston Two died a brutal death at the age of thirtytwo, it seemed as though the Harrison luck had expired.

This chapter of my family history is downplayed in father's book. Nonetheless, I found it to be completely mesmerizing. I remember the great relief I felt when I learned that I was not the first ne'erdowell in the family.

I was sure my father thought of me in this way. Regardless, I eventually figured out the full story, which went like this:

Winston Two's battered corpse was pulled from the Saginaw Bay in the spring of 1891. Father had included a single newspaper clipping about this in his book. In it, the county coroner proclaimed the death to have been accidental. Winston had been missing for five days before his corpse was found. The coroner speculated that a fall from the family sailboat caused the bruises that covered his body. I doubted this, so I researched the incident by reading follow-up articles from that time. I found out that most people believed Two had been kidnapped and murdered while visiting Bay City's Catacombs.

The Catacombs was a notorious waterfront playground that catered to the gamblers, lumberjacks, ship hands, prostitutes, and ruffians that populated Michigan's Lower Peninsula during the lumber era. Winston Two had been well known in the whorehouses and gambling dens. The patrons of these establishments claimed that a gang surrounded him, hog-tied him, and dragged him to the river where they beat him to death. Most said it was to settle an unpaid gambling debt. This was not mentioned in my father's book.

Nonetheless, Winston Two died and after his funeral Winston the First adopted Two's eleven-year-old son, whom he simply called Three. Winston the First was seventy-six years old then. He also took Two's spouse, Lucinda, as his own. She was twenty-eight. The unlikely trio quietly relocated to Birmingham as venomous gossip stirred behind them. Fortunately, the adoption was propitious. Three was receptive to Winston's financial instruction.

In his late teens, Three met a young man in Detroit named Henry. Henry was the creative type, always tinkering with things, inventing this and building that. He and Three quickly became close friends.

One hot summer's night the two traveled to Belle Isle to enjoy frosted mugs of cold Stroh's beer. During the course of the evening Henry told Three about a horseless carriage – he called it an automobile – which he was hoping to build.

This idea fascinated Three and he took it to Winston the First, who offered to support Henry's research in exchange for a one-tenth ownership of Henry's fledgling company. Five years later Three's wife, Penelope, gave birth to my father, Winston Four. By then the family fortune had increased tenfold. Two months later, Winston the First passed away and his ownership in Henry's company passed to Three.

Much to Three's delight, my father was another financial prodigy. At the age of thirty-two, Four was named Chairman of the Board for Henry's motor company, a position he held during this fateful summer. His place on the Board, combined with his financial aptitude, is why we still had the wealth first created by Winston the First.

But that's only part of the story: the money part. My family's emotional history didn't have the same happy ending. I think that's the price of wealth. Sadly, my father also inherited some of Two's bad luck. When my father was twenty-one his first-born son and my brother, Winston Five, died at birth, nearly killing my mother Elizabeth in the process. Neither fully recovered from this loss. My father buried himself in his work; my mother immersed herself in charitable causes.

Three years later my sister Olivia was born, and four years after that I arrived. My parents didn't seem to notice. It was as though neither of us could replace our dead brother. This was particularly true for my father. My mother tried to love us. Still, there was emptiness within her that we could both see.

Father's outright rejection affected us differently. Olivia wanted his love and acceptance, so she excelled academically, socially, and athletically. Her effort was

barely rewarded. Four tolerated her presence and acknowledged her achievements, at best. I was much more
passive and didn't even try to gain his favor. I could see it
was hopeless. I was not disappointed.

My father interpreted my passivity as a lack of moti-
vation, and I suppose he was right. To be motivated you
need to work toward a reward you value and feel is ob-
tainable. I wanted his attention, of course - all sons do. I
just didn't think I'd get it even if I tried. All I could hope
for was that someday, when I was grown, I might earn his
respect.

When I was twelve I was sent to the Western Reserve
Academy, a prep school outside of Cleveland. My seven
years there were notable for two reasons. First, I became
the only student in the Academy's history to receive every
disciplinary and academic punishment known to exist and
still graduate. In addition, I earned All-American honors
as a swimmer my senior year, which unquestionably in-
fluenced their decision to let me graduate. My father was
so displeased with my academic and social struggles that
he ignored my swimming accomplishments.

Needless to say, I avoided being alone with my father.
But I couldn't do that all the time. During this summer I
spent time with him alone on the first Saturday of June. I
did not know about this until Bradford, our butler, called
me to dinner.

◆◆◆

"Your mother and sister are attending a Garden Club
function this evening, so the gentlemen will dine together," he announced. "Dinner is served."

Yuck, I thought to myself. As always dress was formal, which I thought was ridiculous. We arrived
simultaneously, nodded a greeting to each other, and ate
quickly and quietly. The mood was strained. After dessert
and coffee was served he released Bradford and the cook
for the evening. The grand house grew quieter, which I
didn't think was possible. We finished our dessert and va-

cated the mute formal dining room, both drawn to the lake, coffee cup and saucer in hand.

We moved to the verandah overlooking Little Traverse Bay and settled into comfortable white-wicker rockers. The twilight that evening cast a vibrant glow upon the boathouse in front of us. The slow, steady lapping of the waves accented the mood. Then, against my fervent hushed wishes, my father spoke to me.

"Cole," he began, "I know how much you love this country, how much you enjoy being up north." I said nothing. I actually preferred Birmingham, although I rarely spent time there. I knew better than to disagree with him because in his mind he was never wrong, and when he was he would never admit it.

"I suppose," I obediently replied.

"I've been giving your future a lot of thought lately," he continued. "It occurs to me that we can kill two birds with one stone. After all, once you've won the Olympic Gold Medal you will want to start working for the family."

Again I was offended by his assumption. I was focused upon my college career, not the Olympics. We had discussed the Olympics once before and I told him then that for me to even qualify for the team was a stretch. My father disagreed; he assumed I would win Olympic Gold. He said Harrison men were bred to succeed. I was not so sure. After all, Winston Two was a Harrison man wasn't he? I didn't remind father of that fact.

I had qualified for the Olympic Trials though, which I felt was accomplishment enough. I was nationally ranked in only one event, the 60-yard Freestyle, which they did not swim at the international level; I was not ranked in any international events. Despite this I felt I had an outside chance in the Freestyle relay. Six swimmers would qualify for it, four of which would swim in the finals. The problem was that it was an 800-meter relay, meaning that I would have to swim a 200-meter leg -almost four times longer than my best race. I would also try to qualify in the 100-meter Freestyle, although that was a longer shot: only the top three finishers made the team. They did not have 4x100 Freestyle Relay in 1950.

If I had to state an Olympic goal, it was to simply make the team. That would be a tremendous achievement, even if my father did not recognize that fact. Regardless, the Olympics were two years away. Michigan State was my immediate focus. My desire was to be successful in college, which was why I was working out six days a week in the White Pine Inn swimming pool: longer races required greater endurance and college was full of longer races.

I also took offense at father's assumption that I would want to work for the family. That had never been discussed, and was not my intent. As usual, Four assumed that what he wanted was what I wanted.

"I hadn't really thought about that, Father," I replied honestly. Four ignored my response, continuing as if I hadn't spoken.

"You've seen how this area has grown since you first came north. When your grandfather bought this cottage it was even more remote. It took him two days just to get here. Even now it's a full day's drive," he said.

"It is a haul," I agreed.

"That it is," Four nodded. "And I have inside knowledge that the travel time to get here will change in a few years, when the new interstate opens. I've been told that project will be approved. Once that's built you'll be able to get here in hours. That means millions of people will drive here to escape the cities."

"I suppose they will, Father," I agreed.

"You're damn right they will! And they'll need to stay somewhere," Four concluded. "That's why I've got an option to buy some Indian land north of here. We're going to build over a hundred and fifty pre-fabricated two-bedroom houses on it. I want you to run this project for me, after you win your Olympic Gold. You'll live up here and sell those homes for me."

"Why me?" I asked suspiciously.

"Why you? Think, Cole, think," Four spat. "Try to use that head of yours for something other than a showcase for expensive dental care. First, I work in Detroit. I can't be here. Second, after your Olympic win everybody will want to buy a house from you, no matter where or what it is. Third, your name will add two grand to the profit of every home we sell. It's good business Cole."

"You would know, Father," I muttered. This seemed to satisfy the man, so I excused myself, left the verandah, changed clothes and left the cottage. My time with him was done; I was off to see Kate.

KATE

Cole and I met at the Juilleret's that night. While eating our after-dinner ice cream, Cole told me about his father's idea.

"That's great news, Cole. You could build a wonderful house for us," I exclaimed without thinking. He fell silent and I knew I'd misspoken. Until that moment I had successfully avoided talking to him about our future. I knew it was considered presumptuous for a local to even imagine ending up with someone from the Point. I braced myself for his response to this embarrassing indiscretion. I was so stupid sometimes.

"Sure, I suppose it's a good idea, Kate. Some of Four's are," Cole replied nonchalantly, ignoring my faux pas. "But can you honestly see me living up here year-round? I mean really, this burg's too small for me."

I was both saddened and relieved. I looked past him, through the large picture window and to his Buick Roadster convertible parked outside. I realized that his silence was not caused by my slip of the tongue. He was lost in thought over his relationship with his father. I wondered how much of Cole's reluctance to embrace his father's business proposal was personal. Most of it, I suspected. I knew they did not get along. Cole's car symbolized this chasm.

Four resented Cole's choice of automobile, which had been Cole's intent. After his prep school graduation Four reluctantly agreed to buy Cole a car, despite his disappointment with Cole's academic and social performance. I'm sure Four intended for the car to be one of Henry's; after all, he was the Chairman of Board. But Four did not dictate this condition, so Cole seized the opportunity and selected the sleek, fast, sporty Roadster, fire red with white interior. The fact that it was built by a rival made it most appealing. To Four's credit he bought Cole the car anyway, honoring his word. I suspect he knew there would better ways to teach Cole the meaning of loyalty.

Cole began to slide his chair out, intent on leaving the table. I wanted to keep the evening positive, so I quickly huddled up to him and nibbled his ear seductively. Then I whispered to him.

"How about I show you what this burg offers!" Cole raised his eyebrows and smiled. He put his arm around me and kissed my forehead.

"Discretion Kate, discretion," he replied. I playfully slapped his arm.

"Not that you scamp, that's all mine. I'm talking about this." I handed him the Harbor Festival flyer, and pointed to a new featured event.

"North Country Swim Championship," he read aloud. "Interesting. It says here that it will be a three-mile open water swim. I swim a mile just for warm-ups. I could win this easy."

"Really?" I asked excitedly. I had never seen him race.

"You bet. This is great Kate!" His effervescence was growing. "I'm focusing on endurance this summer. That's what I need for college. This gives me a goal to work towards! That will help me stay motivated."

With his mood improved we playfully flirted for another hour, and I never again mentioned our future. Later, as the staff began to close the family restaurant, I hugged him tightly, kissed him deeply, and began to leave.

"I've got to run now, hon. I'm working breakfast tomorrow and I need my beauty sleep," I said reluctantly. "Maybe we can go and check out the land your father's talking about sometime soon? See it once, and then decide. Your father will accept your decision better if you do."

I embraced him a final time and gently tongued his earlobe. Breaking away from him I added, "I hear it's pretty remote out there." Then I winked, pausing briefly to linger and gaze into his attentive blue eyes. Finally I turned and walked away, tossing my long blond hair as I left the bar.

AUPETCHI

Our annual celebration was winding down. My ritual swim had gone well, although the water had been predictably cold. Luckily, it was also calm, so I made good time.

The citizens of the north village joyfully celebrated my arrival with ritual feasts and ancestral dances. My appearance ensured continued unity and prosperity for the Anabe. We had survived another harsh winter. Our resolve remained strong, and *Memegot* symbolized this reality.

My favorite activity that week was the telling of our past. Our history has always been passed down orally. One night of *Memegot* was spent doing just that, in front of a huge campfire. Because our past is so important to this story, I will tell you what I know. Then I can continue with the events of the summer we speak of.

Before establishing a permanent settlement here we lived at the south end of the great lake Michi Gama. We called our village Shegogong. We lived where the *waubesh* city Chicago now sits. Even then we visited Tawkenin every summer, just as the *waubesh* do to this day. We traveled north from our winter villages to cultivate a variety of crops, and to hunt for game, and harvest fish, both of which were abundant. The region was so fertile that our elders decided that we should move there permanently, which we did more than three hundred and fifty years ago. It was then that the twin villages were settled.

Not long after relocating to Tawkenin, the first *waubesh* appeared from the northeast, landing at the strategic Straits of Mackinac. Over the years, three different fortified trading posts were built there. Tawkenin was far enough away to be considered tactically unimportant, so they did not settle in our region. Still, the posts were close enough to concern our warriors, especially since they were embroiled in one war after another.

Miraculously, we sided time and again with the victorious army. First we allied ourselves with the French, who appeared in 1634. Then, more than a hundred years later, we aligned with the British. Finally we sided with the colonists in their battle with Great Britain, colonists who later become the Americans. As a result, the north village and the south village remained unspoiled and were rich in native tradition and culture, as they were when this summer began.

Our ability to ally wisely ensured our continued existence. The *waubesh* who settled the Mackinac region to the north stayed away from our land. All was well, until a different group of *waubesh* arrived from the south. They came on steamboats and created the village called Harbor Springs, which led to the events that resulted in *Memegot.*

So you can see that *Memegot* was one of our newer celebrations. When it first began we honored the Good News with a one-day feast. Aushegun's legendary swim was not reenacted then, for no one dared match his aquatic prowess. No one, that is, until my great-great-grandfather Audawmeg. He changed all that. His story was the one I loved to hear the most.

When he was fifteen summers old, Audawmeg joined a fishing party that canoed to our most revered Michi Gama fishing grounds. They traveled south to an area made sacred by a mother bear and her cubs. Tradition tells how long ago a forest fire raged in what is now Wisconsin, making food scarce for a mother bear and her two cubs. Fearing for their safety, she led them on a long swim across Michi Gama to escape the flames and search for sustenance. They swam more than fifty miles, leaving from the western shore and heading east.

The mother bear, whom we call Mishe Mokwa, reached the eastern shore and collapsed on the beach, exhausted from her ordeal. She had just enough strength left to raise her head and look across the water for her cubs. The youngsters had lagged far behind, however, and could not be seen. Soon Mishe Mokwa fell asleep. Her cubs continued to struggle as they approached shore. Finally, too young and too weak to endure, they drowned a few miles offshore, under the light of the moon.

Mishe Mokwa eventually woke and continued to wait for them, refusing to move until they arrived safely. Sadly, they never did. To this day Mishe Mokwa still watches and waits for her cubs. A mountain of sand covers her now, which the *waubesh* call Sleeping Bear Dune. The Anabe believed that Manitou was so impressed by her loyalty that he created two islands where the cubs perished, called the Manitou Islands. We believed that the waters surrounding these islands possessed Mishe Mokwa's spirit. Her sorrow and hopelessness cloaked the region. Consequently we did not inhabit it, out of respect. Instead we camped on the islands, fished the waters, harvested our catch, gave sincere thanks, and left.

The fishing party that included Audawmeg was doing just that. They speared fish in the dark of night, attracting them to their canoes by lighting giant torches attached to the bows. One night while they were out, Grandfather Thunder spoke abruptly and loudly. His voice was strong. Fast moving clouds quickly shadowed the waning moon. The wind blew violently. Bolts of lighting pierced the sudden, driving rain. Audawmeg's canoe was overturned as it raced to shore and six men fell into the turbulent water.

Mishe Mokwa must have seen the struggling men because her spirit filled Audawmeg. Suddenly he swam with the endurance of a whitefish and the power of a sturgeon, heroically saving himself and his five comrades while the storm's fury raged about them.

After the storm passed the fishermen returned to their village and told the people what happened. A council was called and the elders concluded that Audawmeg's gift was his ability to swim. They honored him by appointing him Odawgen, and by adding the ceremonial swim to *Meme-got*, which extended the celebration period. And so the tradition continued for five generations, into the summer I speak of now.

As Odawgen, I was prohibited from reading what I carried, as were all the Anabe. Only Sawmay could read and reveal the content. Consequently, as I prepared for my return to the south village only the citizens of the north village knew that I carried the Harbor Festival flyer. Even so, they did not understand what it meant.

Sawmay alone understood the document's significance. This was because our ancestors came to him in a dream and told him that I must swim in the Harbor Festival Race. They did not tell him why. I learned of Sawmay's dream on my fourth night in the north village.

Late that evening, Sawmay had summoned me to his *wigwom*. His lodge was warm and smoky when I arrived, a small fire blazed within. Sawmay sat quietly as I entered and settled myself across from him on the dirt floor, the fire between us. I reverently crossed my legs and bowed my head slightly. Sawmay took a piece of kindling from the fire and lit a long and ornate pipe, then inhaled deeply from it. He handed the pipe to me. As I smoked, I admired the finely carved image that served as the bowl; Manitou's likeness returned my gaze. I gave the pipe back to Sawmay. Minutes passed. Finally, he spoke.

"*Pesendoweshin*," implored Sawmay. He spoke in the Anabe tongue, asking me to listen closely. I assume few of you are familiar with it, so I will translate from here on in.

"I will listen to you," I replied.

"The *waubesh* continue to threaten our existence. They encroach upon our land each and every summer. Always trying to take a little more," Sawmay frowned, "despite our agreement." I remained respectfully silent, waiting for him to continue.

"They have wicked hearts and I fear their desire is to take our villages, to steal our land," he added. "This disgusts me." Sawmay spit as he uttered the last statement, showing his contempt.

"I too am disgusted," I said. "But what are we to do, Sawmay? Can we ever convince them to leave us alone forever?"

"I used to believe we could not, that they would inevitably move onto our lands and force us to leave. But today I am not so sure," the wise man declared. "This is why I called you here. I believe Manitou has selected you, to use your swiftness and strength to secure our homes forever. He has given you the chance to alter our path."

"Me? But I am strong and swift only in the water," I argued. "On land I am slower than the others. And I am not a warrior."

Sawmay re-lit the pipe and took another long toke. Again he passed it to me and I inhaled deeply. We sat silently a while longer. Then Sawmay handed me the flyer promoting the Harbor Festival that I had unknowingly brought to him. He pointed to a section in the corner that read:

NEW THIS YEAR
NORTH COUNTRY SWIMMING
CHAMPIONSHIP!
TO THE VICTOR GOES THE SPOILS.
CLAIM THE TITLE AS THE
FASTEST MAN IN THE LAKE.

I read the flyer and gave the elder a quizzical look. "This does not say anything about Tawkenin. It does not say that the *waubesh* will leave our lands untouched," I began. "How can you be sure that my swimming will ensure that they will leave us alone?"

"You cannot hide from Manitou," was all he offered in reply. I paused to reflect further. I could make little sense of this riddle, but I knew that I must do as Sawmay asked. He had added another pine log to the fast burning fire. As it ignited, I made my reply.

"What you say is true," I acknowledged. "Like you, I trust in Manitou. I have chosen to follow his path, the path of my ancestors. And so I will do as you say. I must go now to prepare myself for this task."

"Be victorious," he said

"Yes," I promised, "I will win." As I left I considered his request. Obviously, I would swim the race, and with Manitou's help I could win. Still, I did not share Sawmay's blind faith that this would stop the *waubesh* from taking our land. He had not shown me how this would protect Tawkenin. Despite my confidence in Sawmay and my faith in Manitou, I suspected that the *waubesh* would never leave. They had been here too long.

I couldn't get this worry to leave my head, even as I prepared to return to the south village. Try as I might, I couldn't help but believe that the *waubesh* would eventually steal Tawkenin. My ability to swim would have little impact upon this reality, despite Sawmay's dream. Still, the memory of my evening with Sawmay inspired me. I vowed that I would fulfill the wise man's desire, and I prayed for Manitou's intervention.

With the sun high above me I packed the flyer in my waterproof pouch and committed Sawmay's response to memory. When I arrived in the south village I would share it with the people.

I moved to the water's edge, where the peoples of the north village quickly surrounded me. Shouts of encouragement accompanied me as I entered Michi Gama. I gave thanks once more to Manitou and began my swim back to the south village.

"Maybe," I thought as I fell into my rhythmic stroke, "Sawmay is right. Maybe Manitou does move in mysterious ways."

Chapter Three

FULL MOON

Sunday, June 11

COLE

I remember the day vividly: it was the first full moon of the summer. I'm not sure if the moon was affecting me, but I felt like a champion both in and out of the pool. Kate and I had spent five of the past eight nights together. We had rambled through the North Country with the top down in my convertible Roadster, watching the moon get bigger and fuller. Each night, the sky had been clear and the air warm and comfortable. It was early summer, so most of the insects were dormant, and the leaves were newly green. The sun set around ten. Dusk lingered past eleven. About the only thing we hadn't done was go to see the land my father had spoken about. I just didn't want to ruin the mood.

Yesterday we had enjoyed a typical evening. Bradford had packed us a thick wool blanket, a six-pack of Stroh's long necks, a pound of smoked whitefish, a loaf of fresh baked bread, and a jar of local cherry preserves. These supplies tucked neatly into the Buick, we let our hearts guide us as we explored some of the fire roads that were carved into the thick north woods. One wound itself through pine and birch, cut across a pristine meadow, and ended at an empty Lake Michigan beach. Another led to a small lake fed by a slow-moving river. For the first time, I really saw and appreciated northern Michigan's natural beauty. It was a world Kate had often told me about but I never understood, until that night. We stopped by the river, threw down the blanket and enjoyed a midnight picnic. I cannot remember ever being happier.

I was equally inspired in the swimming pool, where I had found the elusive "feel" for the water. My endurance was improving and I was swimming consistent intervals. My starts and turns felt explosively powerful. My technique was flawless, and I had never felt stronger. I was primed. And all the credit went to my sister, Olivia, who was coaching me.

I mentioned earlier that Olivia had excelled athletically, earning collegiate All-American honors at Skidmore
College. She was why I swam. When we were young I always went wherever Olivia went, did whatever Olivia did.

This turned out to be a fortunate circumstance since
Olivia took good care of me. She was protective, yet loving. And she was a very good role model. She joined the
local swim team when she was twelve, so I did too. We
both became very good swimmers, and now Olivia was a
very good coach.

Anyway, one thing that sticks out about this day in
particular was that the full moon rose before dusk, and I
could see it as I finished my late-afternoon workout. It
hung in the sky just above Olivia's shoulder, as she stood
poolside.

"Nice workout, Cole," she said. "That was impressive."
I had just finished swimming four sets of ten swims. Each
swim was 200 yards long. I had descended, or reduced my
time, for each set of ten. After the second set the fatigue
was so overwhelming I almost quit. Then I got a second
wind and completed the remaining sets.

"I can't believe how good that felt," I replied after
catching my breath.

"You hit the proverbial wall, Cole, and then swam
right through it. That's the sign of a champion," Olivia declared. Then she directed me to swim down, which I did.
After a shower and a shave, I went home and had a quick
plate in the kitchen with Bradford. That evening I was to
meet Kate once again.

KATE

I anxiously waited for Cole to arrive. I was looking forward to this evening more than most. Not that I didn't enjoy every night with Cole - I did. It's just that this night was special because we were going to an Anabe Pow Wow at Crooked Tree. The event purposefully coincided with the full moon. May had told me that this was so the spirits of the departed grandmothers would be able to join the people.

May and I met when we were in the third grade, when she started going to the Anglo school. She told us all that we should call her May, short for Maymegwan, which meant butterfly. All the other children laughed except me; I thought it was a beautiful name and told her so at recess. We became friends at that moment.

Now, nine years later, I knew quite a bit about the Anabe because of her. More than most white people, that's for sure, and much, much more than Cole. I hoped tonight would encourage him to learn more so that he could appreciate their innate beauty as I did. I knew it was a long shot, but he had recently shared that he appreciated Michigan's natural beauty for the first time. So, you never know. Maybe the full moon was influencing him.

May invited us because she was going to dance in the evening's celebration. I was thrilled when she asked us — well, asked me, actually. She didn't say Cole should come, but she didn't say he couldn't. And I suspected she knew I would ask him. Predictably, he was less than enthusiastic about it. When he picked me up he immediately expressed his disdain.

"Kate," he asked, "tell me why we want to waste our time watching a bunch of Indians dance?"

"May is my best friend and I promised her I'd be there," I explained before adding, "and they call themselves Anabe, or 'the people'."

"I know she's a good friend, Kate," he scoffed, "but really, she's nowhere, man."

"On the contrary, Cole," I said, stiffening as I spoke. "May is a wonderful friend. She's taught me so much, like the meaning of friendship and commitment."

"Yeah, yeah, okay," Cole mellowed, "we'll go. We can check out our future home site while we're at it."

"Say what?" I asked, startled by his comment.

"Our future home site. I heard what you said that night at the Juilleret's you know," he replied. "The Indians – no, make that 'the Anabe' · live on the land my old man has the deed to."

"Cole, you never told me that," I protested, horrified. "You just said it was up north a bit. You never said that it was their land. They're not selling any that I know of."

"It is up north a bit isn't it?" he reasoned with shrug. "I didn't think it mattered, since they can't sell what they don't own."

With that, Cole put the pedal to the metal and the Buick roared off into the evening, driving north, along the lakeshore. The night was beautiful but I barely noticed. I sat quietly next to him, troubled. I looked past him to the west and caught a glimpse of the sun sinking into the freshwater sea. To the east the full moon sat suspended high in the evening sky. A cool breeze blew in off Lake Michigan, carrying the humidity of the day away with it.

Soon the timberland enveloped us as we traveled along County Road 119. Deep blue and green spruce trees dominated the coniferous forest, contrasted at times by bright white birch and dull gray maple. In the distance sang a Kirtland Warbler, luring potential mates to its lair. To this point I had been stunned by Cole's revelation so I had remained silent. Finally I broke the silence with a whisper.

"Tawkenin."

"What's that, babe?" Cole asked.

"Tawkenin," I repeated. "That's what the Anabe call

it. It means home, or native land. You can't build on the Anabe homeland, Cole. And I certainly won't live there. It's just not right."

"Whatever," Cole muttered indifferently. I could tell that he wasn't going to discuss this now. My head throbbed as I tried to understand my conflicted emotions, but I found it hard to concentrate. Cole had said something about 'our' house, which proved that he was considering a future together. What could be better than that?

At the same time, his father - and possibly he - had apparently obtained legal rights to the Anabe land. I knew white people historically stole Indian land all the time. I just couldn't believe he would do it too. For Winston Four, yes, I could fathom it; he was without scruples. But I expected so much more from Cole.

I knew how much the Anabe revered Tawkenin. I simply could not conceive of making my best friend and her family move from their homeland. What could be worse than this? I prayed that somehow, some way, Cole would never build there. If he did, I could not live there with him.

Needless to say, when we arrived at the Pow Wow I was out of sorts. But I forced myself to forget my troubles and put on a happy face for the evening, for May's sake. I could at least ensure that her night remained special.

AUPETCHI

Our annual Pow Wow was another favorite of mine. There I could display the handiwork of my greatest passion: sculpture. Now don't misunderstand me. The greatest honor of my life was being named Odawgen, to carry on the work of my ancestors. I filled that role with a great sense of duty. But it was just that: an obligation, a responsibility. Sculpture, on the other hand, was a choice, and source of great personal pleasure. It was my time, serving only my dreams.

I started as a little boy, whittling small pieces of wood into animal figures. Gradually I moved away from wood and ended up working solely on pieces of fossilized coral found scattered along the shore of Michi Gama. You probably know it as a Petoskey stone. At least, that's what May told me the *waubesh* called it. They say that the waters of Michi Gama were once part of a giant freshwater sea that covered all of what is now Michigan - and most of Ontario. Beneath the surface of this sea there loomed a gigantic coral reef. The great sea eventually receded, leaving behind the Great Lakes and, in this part of the world, the fossilized remains of this coral.

However it got here, I venerated this Petoskey stone. I worked it with absolute reverence, creating from it images of the wolf, brook trout, crane, deer, sturgeon, and fox. I chose these creatures because we admired them greatly. Like many native nations, we believed in three worlds existing together and in balance: the sky world, the surface world, and the underneath world. In their own unique way these creatures connected us to these worlds. Plus, they each modeled qualities we admired.

The crane possessed the gift of flight and so moved close to the sky world. The sturgeon was a bottom feeder, connecting us to the underneath world. We honored the wolf because of the fidelity he had to his mate, and the loyalty he had to his pack. We revered the brook trout because it was tenacious in battle and the fox because of its cunning. The deer was significant not only because it provided an abundant food source for my people, but also because we cherished its grace and eloquence.

Many people admired my work. I think it was because it was intricate yet simple, if that makes sense. I gave most of my work as gifts to special people I met in life. I also sold a few at the annual Pow Wow. I knew the *waubesh* would give me many coins and paper for my work, coins and paper that I would exchange for the supplies only the *waubesh* sold.

The moon was already shining brightly above us, while the last rays of an orange sunset reflected off a wisp of clouds. I was sitting with May behind a hand-hewn cedar table that had some of my carvings on it. May shared the display space, selling some of the porcupine quill jewelry she had made. She did beautiful work and I was proud that she carried on this native tradition. We noticed a *waubesh* couple approaching us, arms linked. It was May's friend Kate and her boyfriend.

"Kate, you made it," May exclaimed as she recognized her friend. "*Pindigayn*. Welcome." "Of course I did," Kate said as May rose to embrace her. "I wouldn't miss it for anything. Now when do you dance?" "In about twenty minutes," May explained. "We're going to do the Raccoon Dance."

I got up from the table and nodded to Kate, whom I knew, before awkwardly offering my right hand to her man. I knew this was a *waubash* greeting.

"I am called Aupetchi," I said.

"Hey chief," her man responded, "I'm Cole Harrison. Nice to see you. Are you the cat who carved all the trinkets?"

"I created the carvings, yes," I answered politely.

His terminology did not offend me since I knew that most *waubesh* could not see the spirit living within the stone.

"Are you with this good woman?" I said as I bowed to Kate.

"Thank you Aupetchi," Kate interjected with a notice-able blush. "It is a pleasure to see the mysterious *wesemaw* of my best friend once again."

"Weseesaw who?" Cole interrupted. "What kind of gibberish are you speaking here?" Kate reprimanded him quickly.

"It's not gibberish Cole, it's their language. *Wesemaw* means brother. Aupetchi is May's brother, and a highly regarded Anabe."

"Why? Because he carves trinkets out of Petoskey stones?" Cole asked incredulously.

"No Cole, because he is Odawgen, the messenger," Kate explained impatiently.

"Oh, of course, the messenger," Cole sarcastically re-plied. "Well, messenger, I'll take this wolf off your hands."

"You are interested in the wolf spirit?" I said, ignoring the obvious tension in the air. "He is revered among my people. He is faithful to his purpose on the surface world. This makes him difficult to hunt. He will show himself to you only when he must sacrifice his spirit for you. You must earn his respect first."

"Yeah, right," Cole sneered.

"My apologies," I replied while removing the effigy from the table. "Wolf is not for sale. He will be given only as a gift, from me to a strong spirit. To someone I re-spect." Cole bristled at my response.

"We understand, Aupetchi," Kate answered. She tried to diffuse the situation by telling me that my works were beautiful.

"Thank you," I said. Then she turned to May, hoping to change the subject.

"Now tell me all about the Raccoon Dance, May." Maymegwan took the bait.

"The Raccoon Dance honors the gifts raccoon gives to our people. In it we imitate their mating ritual. We have

seen that the male chases the female while courting, being sure to never touch her until she has approved of his
advances. In this dance I will be a female and you will see
many males take their turn trying to win my favors," she
explained.

"And who will you choose?" Kate teased.

"A man who is both gentle and strong," May replied.

"As if," laughed Kate. "Not even the Anabe have a
man who is both. If you do, I will learn the dance too.
Come on Cole, let's leave them alone and get a good seat."

Kate took Cole's arm and led him to the dance circle.
As she looked back to offer May final encouragement, her
gaze met mine briefly. Her eyes softened, as if to say, perhaps such men do exist. I fleetingly held her stare, smiled,
and then redirected a glare towards Cole. As much as I
admired her, I disliked him.

Chapter Four

WANING QUARTER

Monday, June 19

KATE

Despite the shaky start, our night at the Pow Wow had been fun. I loved watching May dance, and much to my surprise, Cole enjoyed himself too. He still didn't think much of Aupetchi, mind you, but we had a good time and that's what mattered most. Or so I thought.

Now, however, it was a week later and things had changed. Cole had been obnoxious to me ever since the Pow Wow. It was as if he needed to punish me all week because he was nice on my night. He could be such a little boy at times.

Not only that, but I was also dead tired. The restaurant's summer season had officially started; all public schools were now closed. The weekend that had just ended had been the busiest yet. And if that wasn't exhausting enough, I hadn't slept in two nights, because a reoccurring nightmare of mine had returned.

First let me address work. I never understood why everyone seems to vacation at the same time, as soon as school ends. Why not spend some time at home first, and then go away?

The crowd in Harbor Springs had been unusually large, which was good for local commerce but tiresome to my "chiseled long legs" as one gentleman had called them. Business at the White Pine had been merciless and I knew the summer rush would only intensify from this day forward, until its Labor Day weekend peak. It always did.

My mother Helen had met with the White Pine staff before the weekend started to motivate us with her annual pep talk. Sometimes she was more of a coach than a manager. She reminded us that eighty percent of Michigan's fifteen million people worked and lived on five percent of the land, most within sixty miles of the state's southern border. Consequently, most of Michigan was uninhabited, unspoiled and accessible to this population.

She explained that the White Pine's potential market included everyone living within five hundred miles of Harbor Springs. This included much of Ohio, Indiana, and Illinois, meaning over sixty million people were within vacation distance. This explained why so many visitors came to northern Michigan every summer. There were a lot of people living nearby who needed to escape.

So they came up north to explore Michigan's natural beaches, sail her energetic waters, hunt her secluded woods, canoe her swift, shallow rivers, and eat at restaurants like the White Pine. Mom urged the staff to prepare to be overwhelmed, but to love every minute of it. The haul had just begun, she reminded us, and stamina was important. I agreed and took her message to heart.

I worked six consecutive twelve-hour days so I needed to rest big-time. Six long days with four nights' sleep just didn't cut it. Fortunately Mom was kind enough to give me this day off. I decided to try and "unlax," a term my father and I learned from the Bugs Bunny cartoons that we watched together when I was a child. It meant both to relax and to unwind. When we did it together we would find a secluded dune on our favorite beach, then hide behind it, undisturbed. I decided to start today by pampering myself with breakfast, so I drove to the south shore of Little Traverse Bay and ate at the State Lunch Diner in Petoskey.

I took my time, slowly enjoying a small bowl of fruit, a cheese omelet, toast with butter, and two cups of coffee with cream. While eating I overheard a conversation that was taking place in the booth in front of me.

"You know," whined a tan, skinny kid who looked like he worked in a marina, "Harrison, Winston Harrison, from the Point. People call him Four. Anyway, his old roommate is a U.S. Senator who is good friends with General Eisenhower, Ike."

"And these cronies are getting together to do what?"

asked his companion, a vibrant, tall bartender I knew, who had worked up north for many summers.

"I already told you. They're hoping to build that damn interstate highway system after Ike is elected President. They might even build a bridge to replace the ferries at Mackinac."

"Really? That's a good idea. I just drove up from Mt. Pleasant and that was a haul. I've read about this inter-state system · it might make it easier to get up here. I saw one plan where it would run all the way from Saulte Saint Marie to Miami."

"Exactly," snorted the boatyard dog. "That's why I'm against it. I don't need any lousy southerners running up here." I suddenly felt even more tired. I knew that more people meant more work. It occurred to me that I might be working at the White Pine forever.

I would grow old early doing that. I felt destined to be an old hag, with varicose veins and wrinkled skin. The physical demands alone would kill me. Double shifts, six days a week, year after year. I knew the routine already: open the restaurant, help prep for lunch, supervise the dining room during lunch while waiting tables, clean up after lunch, help prep for dinner, then waitress the first half of the dinner shift. Catch up on paperwork when pos-sible, it made my head throb. To think of spending the summer doing this was exhausting enough; the idea of spending my life in that rut was downright disheartening.

This depression was compounded when I reflected upon my desire to be with Cole. I doubted that he would ever ask me to marry him. I knew his parents didn't ap-prove of me because I was not their social equal. Sure, he had teased me about it recently, but I was sure it was just that: a tease. Plus, I wasn't even sure I would marry him if he did ask.

I knew in my heart what qualities I wanted my hus-band to have, and I was fairly certain that Cole didn't have them: qualities like integrity, a sense of purpose, and commitment to a life plan. Just thinking about this fried my brain even further. I was so confused. I didn't understand where Cole was coming from and I didn't understand my feelings for him.

As if this was not enough, recently my time with Cole had become tiresome. I no longer found comfort and friendship when I was with him. He no longer gave me enough space. This last hectic weekend was the worst. He had been clingy, demanding and unsupportive. Then, to top it all off, my nightmare had returned. It always seemed to come when I could handle it the least. Clearly it was time to leave the State Lunch. It was time to escape, to unlax. It was time to find bliss.

Fortunately, my family literally lived in Bliss. Bliss, Michigan, that is. My parents, Helen and the late Stan Kilpatrick, told my brothers and me that they decided to settle into the small, isolated village of Bliss because they believed that the name - and so the place - was magical. How cool is that? Of course, such thinking carried a price.

My mother in particular was the subject of much local gossip, especially after my father died. I heard people talk about her throughout my life, even though they tried to hide it from me. She was a bit weird. We could all see that. Much talk centered on how she dressed. Today her style is called "bohemian." It didn't have a name then. She loved long flowing skirts, big blousy tops, bare feet (when she wasn't working) and colorful hats.

My brothers told me she was gossiped about because people were jealous. I wasn't sure I believed them, but they were all older, so I tried. They said that men thought she was crazy because she never remarried after our father died, and the women didn't like her because she tempted their husbands. Now I see that all of this was probably true, but I could not see it then.

I did understand that lots of people were jealous of her success as a restaurant manager. Very few women worked outside the home then; almost none managed a

business. Only my brothers and I recognized and appreciated her professional accomplishments. Everyone else
seemed content to simply critique her personal eccentrici-
ties.

Nonetheless, my brothers and I had great respect for
her. We knew what she had gone through personally,
since we had all dealt with the loss of our father in some
manner. We also understood how she had transformed the
White Pine restaurant. We had all worked with her along
the way. My oldest brother Jack was the first, helping her
when the restaurant was neglected and in disrepair. It
was so bad that even the Inn's guests avoided it. After
Jack came Jim, then Gerry, then Geoff, and finally, me.
Now, some fifteen years later, it was one of the most
popular and talked about restaurants north of Detroit. It
didn't matter who you were or where you were from; the
White Pine was where you wanted to be seen in Harbor
Springs.

This was my fifth season working with mom, my third
as her lunch supervisor. We made an unbeatable team.
Because of that, many locals believed I was eccentric, too.
The corn doesn't fall far from the flake, they'd say. That
made me mad. I hated being judged when they didn't even
know who I really was. Mom didn't care, though, and she
told me to ignore the talk. I tried, but it didn't work. I did
care; I wanted people to know ME and to like ME.

I needed to recharge myself and I knew where to do it.
So I paid my bill, left the Great Interstate Debate behind
me, and drove back to Harbor Springs. When I reached
Main Street I took a moment to look around me as I
waited for the light to change. The morning was clear and
the breeze off the lake was steady: it was a perfect day for
the beach. I drove north on Pleasantview through the
highlands, and entered Bliss. The village was as active as
a community consisting of a general store, post office and
a church can be: not too.

I turned west on Big Trail, which ran into Sturgeon

Road, leading me to our house. The house was only five hundred feet from Bliss Beach, beautiful and isolated. We were far from civilization, living just beyond the north-west border of Tawkenin. In fact, our house stood between Tawkenin and the beach.

I could now find the peace I needed. I could hibernate behind a dune and escape. Be it sunrise, sunset, noon, or midnight, I always found balance when visiting this haven. It was noon by the time I parked the car.

I tossed the keys onto the kitchen table and walked through the house to the mud porch. I paused to apply insect repellent to my exposed legs and arms, and then moved to a partially hidden pathway bordering our acreage. I scampered westward to the beach, following an overgrown trail. Had I scampered east I would have gone through the forest to the heart of Tawkenin. The hidden path was an ancient Anabe trace that was still used today. The Anabe retained beach rights at Bliss.

Before I ducked onto the trace I stole a glance at my bedroom window on the second floor. My curtains were drawn; I had closed them last night when the nightmare returned. It came to me less often now, but it still came, as it had since the night my father, Stanley Gibson Kilpatrick, disappeared when I was fourteen years old. I wondered if it would ever stop. It was always the same.

◆◆◆

I can still remember the last time I saw him alive: he was forty-seven years old. I was hiding behind the pantry door watching him argue with my mother. He was about to finish another season working on a Great Lakes Freighter, which he had done since he was twelve. He was a cook on the *A.L. Baker,* a 740-foot saltie that worked the lakes in the summer and the Caribbean in the winter.

The *A.L. Baker* had run the same route all summer: North from her home port of Rogers City on Lake Huron, through the Straits of Mackinac, then down south 300 Lake Michigan miles to Buffington, Indiana. This was his second season on the *A.L. Baker* and she was scheduled to carry one last load of Rogers City limestone down to Indiana.

My mother pleaded with him. He had worked the range on 45 runs this season and Mom said their savings were flush. They had earned more than enough to survive the long, harsh northern Michigan winter. My father didn't work the off-season, so his year was essentially finished.

"Why not stop now?" my mother begged.

"Helen, you know I promised Captain Bryan I'd finish the season," my father reasoned. "I can't go back on my word. After all, who else can pan-fry perch like me?" Mom laughed, but was not appeased.

"I know, hon, it's the right thing to do. Your word is your honor," she acknowledged. "But I still don't want you to go. I can't explain why, but I feel like this time it's a mistake. I feel it in my heart." Mom paused, then added: "Are you sure the hull is safe?" Two weeks earlier the *A.L. Baker* had run aground near Onekema. The impact ruptured one of her steel hull plates.

"Of course it is, sweets. We wouldn't sail if it wasn't," father answered naively. "It's only one more run, the last run of the year. Then they'll tow her to dry dock and she'll get some certified, state-of-the-art hull plates installed. The mate says they're sinking over a quarter million bucks into her, then it's off to the Caymans."

"Alright then. If you feel sure you'll be safe, go," mom reluctantly agreed. I never saw him again.

◆◆◆

I darted down the path, arrived at Bliss Beach and quickly located a suitable dune. I ducked behind it, spread out the wool blanket I had carried with me from the car, and laid down. Soon the repetitive murmur of the waves put me blessedly to sleep.

I didn't awaken for hours. When I did it was nearly dark. I sat up and hugged myself, warding off the cool night air.

AUPETCHI

I felt such a sense of responsibility. I knew I had to win this race for my people, although I still did not know why, or for that matter how. No one was permitted to challenge Odawgen, so I had never raced before. That was a sacred position, not an athletic title. It was earned by character, not prowess. This reality troubled me, so early this morning I had paddled my birch bark canoe to Sawmay's home - in the north village. Before I left I greased my skin to keep the mosquitoes and black flies away.

When I arrived Sawmay greeted me warmly and suggested that we walk together. We ambled aimlessly for a while, each quietly pondering the riddle of how to win. There was no need to speak as we both grasped the complexity of the quandary before us. Eventually, Sawmay broke the silence. He had considered the challenge before us and told me that I needed to find the answer elsewhere. He said I should go to Michi Gama and let the spirit of Audawmeg find me. Sawmay believed Audawmeg would show me the way. Today, he said, was a very good day to do this. I agreed and thanked the wise man for his guidance, and immediately headed to the great water.

I moved quickly and quietly along the primitive trace that led from the north village to Michi Gama. The trace meandered through the thick forest and past the *waubesh* family home that sat just outside Tawkenin. I paused when I got to the house. The woods concealed me so I discretely searched the landscape for my sister's friend who lived there. I froze when I saw her standing on a small mud porch. She leaned over and caressed her lean, tan legs.

I assumed she was applying insect repellent, as I had, and thought that it would be sad to be a mosquito right about now: such beauty made inaccessible. I smiled at this fancy as I looked longingly at the shape of her newly moist legs. Extraordinary, I thought to myself.

My eyes drifted upward. I admired her firm, full bosom, and then looked directly into her deep green eyes. She appeared tense, which somehow made her naturally pleasant face even more beautiful. She was the most exquisite *waubesh* woman I had ever seen, which continued to baffle me when I considered the company she kept.

I believe that natural harmony exists in all things, and that the quality of one's spirit is important. I knew that the *waubesh* did not understand this principle, did not agree that one's spirit was particularly relevant. I believed Kate had a radiant soul and that Cole Harrison did not. Their spirits were not harmonious; they were clearly not compatible, yet they were a couple. I did not understand why this enchanting woman found such an aberrant man appealing.

Disheartened, I left the breathtaking view and continued my pilgrimage. I walked for hours along the beach, hoping Audawmeg's spirit would find me as I roamed the sandy lakeshore mulling over the upcoming race. The image of Kate's legs no longer clouded my mind. Finally, as the sun started to set, I scaled a remote sand dune, hoping to rest. A bright carroty hue colored the horizon. I was physically exhausted and spiritually discouraged.

As I ducked behind a dune I saw a woman's silhouette in the distance. She was hugging herself, obviously trying to stay warm. I immediately knew it was Kate. She sat about forty feet away from me, seemingly unaware of my presence. Her cheeks sparkled in the twilight and I could see that she had been crying. Unsure of what to do I sat quietly for many minutes. I decided to ignore her, still trying to find Audawmeg's spirit.

Eventually I concluded that I would not find the guidance I sought. It was when I rose to return to Sawmay that Kate spoke.

"Aupetchi, is that you?" she said. "It's me, Kate Kilpatrick."

"It is I," I replied, "how are you? And why are you out here, alone?"

"I come here all the time," Kate answered. "I love it when I am alone, although tonight is a little chilly."

"Yes," I agreed, "it is cold. Is it the cold that makes you cry?" I regretted this intrusion immediately so I quickly changed the subject. "Would you like a fire?" I asked.

"That's a good idea," she sniffed. I left to quickly gather kindling. When I returned I tried to avoid looking into her soulful green eyes. I busied myself by starting the fire. Despite my best effort, she drew my gaze time and time again as the flames grew. Each time she held my stare, which caused me to avert my eyes in embarrass-ment. Neither of us spoke. We huddled close to the warmth, lost in thought. It pleased me that she appreci-ated the value of silence. I patiently waited for her to speak. Eventually she did.

"Have you ever lost someone you love?" she asked. I paused for a moment before answering.

"I have. My village has lost many good people in my lifetime. I am luckier than many though; my grandfathers and grandmothers all still live. Why, has something hap-pened to this Cole? May says you love him."

"Not him, silly," she scoffed, "he's not lost. In fact he's very easy, too easy, for me to find. Besides, I'm not sure that what I feel for him is really love." Silence again filled the air, interrupted only by the gentle waves rolling against the shore and the sporadic crackle of the fire.

"I only asked because I saw you weeping earlier. Is something else troubling you?" I asked.

"Oh, it's nothing really. I come out here every now and again and think about my father," Kate explained.

"My sister tells me your father is no longer with you," I said. "Is it he who is lost?"

"Yes it is. Your sister is right. May sure tells you a lot about me," she teased.

"Only because I ask many questions," I replied hon-estly, defending my sister's honor.

SHIPWRECK AT SLEEPING BEAR

"Well it's true. My father is with the lake now, right out there as a matter of fact," Kate acknowledged, motioning beyond the shore to the vast, deep lake. A frown came to her face and with it a fresh tear appeared in the corner of her eye.

"I am sorry," I said. After an appropriate period of silence I spoke again. "The lake is a very good place for him to be, I think. In many ways, better than this land we sit upon."

"I know and I thank you," Kate answered before resting her hand upon mine. "I am glad for my father too, he loved this lake. I just miss him terribly. I worry that his death was very painful. In fact, I think I see it in my dreams - his death that is."

"We believe that dreams can show us things we might not otherwise see. Usually with great purpose," I offered.

"I don't see any benefit from this dream. It just makes me sad," she replied.

"Tell me about it. Maybe I can help make sense of it." So she did.

"The dream always begins with my father boarding the A. L. Baker *after a layover in Buffington, Indiana. A strong, consistent wind is blowing and it chills his face. He pulls his watch cap low to his brow and protectively embraces the packages he has with him. I know they are for us, for his family. I also know that the wind has an arctic origin."*

"Dreams are like that, you just know things you never would while awake," she added.

"We see things most clearly when sleeping," I agreed.

"I know," she said, and then continued.

"I can see that my father is uneasy. He pauses at the top of the gangplank and looks closely at his surroundings, as if it will be his last look. It is mid-November and

*dusk shadows the port behind him. The horizon before
him is dark and cloudy. My father whispers the Lord's
Prayer, then exhales deeply and boards the ship."*

"Was he a spiritual man?" I asked.
"Spiritual no, religious yes," she replied.
"I understand," I said.

"Anyway, I see the A.L. Baker *disembark. Then I see
a clock that reads 4:27 and already the sky is pitch black.
My father and his three-man kitchen staff are preparing
the late evening meal and doing some pre-prep for the
next day. I admire his skill as he breads fresh Lake Superior whitefish. Through a porthole I see the lights of
Buffington fade into the darkness.*

*His baker, a family friend named Skip Wilson, ap-
proaches my father cautiously. He knows my father
doesn't like being disturbed while cooking. Outside the
galley I see that the ship is approaching deep open water.
Suddenly it rolls, noticeably. Wind-blown whitecaps vig-
orously attack the hull. I try to warn my father, but of
course he cannot hear me. Then I am back in the galley,
just like that, where Skip and my father are speaking.*

*" 'I'll be right back chief,' Skip says apologetically,
'I've got to change my clothes.'*

"'What? Why? We're just underway!' my father barks.

*" 'Yes sir. I wouldn't go if it weren't necessary. But
look at my shoes and socks, and the legs of my dungarees.
They're all soaked,' Skip explains.*

*" 'Soaked? Why? What did you spill?' my father asks
suspiciously.*

*" 'Nothing Chief. Really, everything's fine: the bread
dough is rising, the biscuits are ready to bake, and the ov-
ens are preheating. It's just that I had to run below deck
to the pantry for some sugar and wheat flour for tomorrow. The cargo tunnel is flooded.'*

" 'Damn it, not again!'

" 'That's right sir,' Skip confirms. 'Except this time, it's not a couple of inches - there's at least a foot of water. On the way up I ran into the watchman. He told me that the hold has a rust hole so big he can see from one compartment into the next.'

" 'Why didn't anybody tell us?' asks my father, clearly frustrated. 'We could lose our entire inventory. Get Hendee and Shutt and empty the cargo pantry. The ship will hold and we've got four more meals to prep. We can't use damaged product.'

" 'Aye, Chief, right away,' Skip replies obediently.

" 'See that you do Wilson, but not until you change your clothes. It's getting cold outside,' my father says, then pauses. 'And Skip, the watchman don't know shit. This old lady can handle a little water aboard.' "

"This dream must be very vivid," I said. "Your detail is impressive."

"It is," Kate agreed. "Of course I've had the dream about fifty times, so I should know it well."

"Then it is the next day. It is early afternoon and Skip Wilson is relaxed and unconcerned. I can see that he believes what my father said. The kitchen crew has prepped, served, and cleaned up three of the voyage's five meals. Dinner is three hours away, so my father has released the kitchen staff for a one-hour break.

"I see my father going to his fo'c'sle cabin where he turns on his short-wave radio. He hears gale warnings posted for all of Lake Michigan. The Coast Guard is directing all lake traffic to port, any port. All lake traffic, that is, but the freighters. The A.L. Baker and her mammoth Great Lakes sisters will not seek shelter; they are big enough to weather any storm, or so it is believed. They forge through ice if they have to. Still, I see the uneasiness my father felt while re-boarding in Buffington return."

"It is as if he senses trouble brewing," I offered.

"Exactly," Kate affirmed. "And because he does, he tries to calm himself."

"In the dream I can hear him think it through. He knows the A.L. Bake*r carries 10,000 tons of water ballast, which reassures him a little. This reduces the chance of her cracking open because of an empty cargo hold. Still, she is traveling light and riding high in the water. The beating she will take by violent waves will be severe. My father looks out of his small porthole, hoping the storm has subsided. Instead, a relentless cold wind gusting up to seventy miles an hour hammers the ship with snow and ice.*

"She alternately rides high on giant swells, then takes a beating from the 35 foot waves that surround her as she settles into their trough. A blinding snow reduces his visibility. He cannot see the ship's bow, which is less than 100 feet away. Doggedly the vessel battles on, slowly moving past the now invisible Manitou Islands. My father cannot calm himself.

"The ship is taking the western route, around the islands and in the open lake, because of her tonnage. The eastern route however, is leeward of the violent storm. Regardless, and somewhat stubbornly, the A.L. Baker *forges ahead per routine. Her Captain has confidence in her strength, her mass and her proven ability to withstand a beating."*

"I don't think I'd be so brave," I interjected. "I have been to the Manitous and I know how dangerous the open water can be."

"I agree Aupetchi, I have thought that over time and again," Kate said. "But this is a freighter, built for such weather. They travel windward all the time."

"I see the hull plates flex as the ship twists in the

breakers. I know this flexibility is a design feature of the freighters, so it doesn't concern me. Then I hear a popping sound. I see sheared rivets shooting away from the hull. As they land, metal on metal, the echo repeats in the empty hold. No one is around to hear this. I know this is not a design feature. Over 300 feet of icy lake water stands between the A.L. Baker and the silent, calm lake bottom, and each lost rivet takes her closer to her destiny."

Kate shuddered and hugged herself tightly. I rose and added more wood to the fire. I stoked the embers and soon a large flame returned. Kate remained silent for many minutes before she started speaking again.

"The clock reads a quarter to six and she is 30 miles southwest of Beaver Island, 12 hours from her winter berth. My father is back at work and begins serving dinner to off-duty wheelmen and deckhands. At 5:49 p.m. a tremendous screech - like fingernails dragging across blackboard, except a 100 times louder - screams through the galley.

"My father drops his ladle into a stockpot of soup and covers his ears. Now, suddenly and completely, he is very concerned. The look of terror on his face is obvious to me. I reach for him, futilely.

"I see him rush up the fore ladder to the pilothouse. Once there he follows the gazes of the Captain Bryan and First Mate Jones through the mist-filled twilight. All are silent. The snowfall has lightened and the aft section is now discernible to the three veteran mariners. The A.L. Baker is listing badly. Clearly, she is taking on water.

"Captain Bryan sounds the general alarm. First Mate Jones orders my father back to the kitchen to secure emergency supplies. En route he hears another thud, louder than the first. The ship lurches, throwing him to the floor. The fore section thrusts upward swiftly and does

not recover. He realizes that the aft sag is much deeper, the damage more violent than imagined. The A.L. Baker *begins to founder. He pulls himself to his feet and hears Captain Bryan thunder instructions to the engine room, his voice echoing from the pilothouse.*

" *'Stop Engines damn it, stop engines now!'*

"The frantic plea of the day officer screaming into the ship-to-shore radio mingles with the Captain's command.

" *'Mayday, mayday, this is the* A.L. Baker *and this is an emergency.'*

"Chaos now reigns. From below he hears a shipmate scream as the icy lake water floods through the rusted hold and into the gangways. I can see that my father knows he cannot get to the kitchen. Instinctively he returns to the pilothouse. Emergency provisions are no longer the priority. Survival is."

"I know how this ends Kate," I said with great sympathy. "You don't need to continue."

"But I must, Aupetchi," she answered. "I believe some good may come from it, and I am tired of carrying it alone in my heart."

"As you wish," I replied. "I will gladly share your burden." She looked into my eyes briefly, gave me a half smile, and then continued.

"At this point I see Captain Bryan fighting to maintain control of the situation.

" *'Grab the life jackets,' he orders.*

" *'We're breaking up,' seconds First Mate Jones.*

"Captain Bryan yanks the ship whistle, giving it seven short tugs and one long blast.

" *'Abandon ship!' he bellows.*

"Then I see my father rushing to escape the horror unfolding before him. He is focused solely on survival. His knows his life will end soon if he doesn't act now, so he struggles to endure. He secures a life jacket from the

gangway and returns to the pilothouse, now high above the heaving sea. He huddles together with six of the crew, including the Captain and Mate, as they withstand the berserk vibrations of a third and final thud. Then they watch in horrific silence as the ship snaps in two."

Kate paused again, and I see tears falling from her eyes. She continued.

"The stern sinks first, exploding in a massive fireball that briefly illuminates the full extent of the damage. The totality of their hopelessness is now obvious. Seconds later the fore section lurches violently and throws my father out of the pilothouse and into the icy lake. His eyes fill with blood as a three-inch gash opens on his forehead. Unable to see, he struggles aimlessly for a few minutes. I can hear the howls of pain and the cries of despair that surround him. He must hear them too. Finally, and I believe knowingly, he takes a last deep breath. He inhales a mixture of oil and water instead of rancid, hot air. Then he slips into unconsciousness, floats for a minute, and sinks below the surface. His time has come."

I sat for a moment in stunned silence. Whatever I say would not be adequate.

"I see," I finally offered. "So coming here to the shore helps you feel close to him, helps you to feel his presence?"

"That's right," Kate replied enthusiastically, despite her sadness. "You understand so quickly. Even though I know he is dead, I believe his spirit lives on here. I just wish Cole could see things so clearly, that he understood how the lake brings me close to him."

"Sometimes the most obvious is the hardest to see," I propose, partially to myself.

We sat together a while longer, gazing into the fast burning fire. Her face took on an azure glow. We become lost in thought. I even wondered if I was dreaming. I thought she might be a vision. It seemed as probable as being here with her.

"So why are you here?" Kate finally asked. "It's late in the evening and you are far from home."

"I am here because like you, I hope to find my ances-tor," I answered.

"How is that? Your parents and grandparents all live," she reasoned.

"This is true. But I wish to find the father of my grandfather. He cannot be found in the villages," I ex-plained.

She considered this for a moment.

"Tell me then," she continued slowly, "why do you look for someone you never knew?"

"That is easy: Because only he can tell me what to do," I said with conviction. "Do you know of the swimmer's race to be held late this summer?"

"Of course I do, Cole is going to win it," she said.

I became mute. I was troubled. Cole's name startled me.

"Are you going to swim also?" she persisted. "May tells me you are very good."

"I have been asked to do so by my people. Sawmay, the wisest of all, tells me that it will help the Anabe. I don't understand why, but he says we will lose our homes if I do not win this race."

"So race," Kate said. "If you're as good as May says you are, you could win the race. May has seen Cole race you know, last year, in Traverse City. May knows what she's talking about."

"It's not the race I fear," I admitted. "You see, my swimming is a special gift, a gift that serves my people. It is also the gift of my ancestor, whose spirit I seek tonight. I think the race might be a trick. I'm afraid that if I race I will lose this gift, even when I win."

She deliberated for a time, and then shook her head with conviction.

"I agree with your elder. You should swim, Aupetchi, and you should beat Cole." Her response stunned me again.

"If you do win, I believe it will help your people. I don't know why, but as we sit here, listening to our ancestors, I am sure of it."

"But how?" I wondered.

"Does that matter?" she answered, then argued. "It seems to me that if we both sense this race has meaning, then you must swim. Sawmay feels that for some reason your winning will preserve Tawkenin forever, which means it will be lost if you don't race. Maybe this race is why you and your ancestor were given the gift of swimming: To help preserve the homes of your people now."

The fire slowly withered. I realized that Kate made sense. My commitment to the match escalated.

"The only question I have for you, Aupetchi, is just how good are you?"

"I am Odawgen, the messenger," I declared, "swift and strong."

"You'd better be swift and strong. And maybe even a little lucky," she grinned.

"I will be," I replied with confidence. "You are very kind."

"As are you Aupetchi, as are you," she said, blushing.

I banked the fire and escorted Kate home. Then I scurried along the trace to the north village, arriving just as dawn broke. I couldn't wait to tell Sawmay that I found the answers I had sought at the lake.

COLE

Kate's decision to spend her rare day off alone puzzled me. I was flustered and disoriented. She had been uncharacteristically distant, almost dejected, and I hoped it was work related. I feared it was not.

Each of our recent evenings together had ended abruptly and poorly, despite my best efforts - ever since the Pow Wow. I had awoken this morning anxious to see her and to make things better. Now that I knew I would not get the chance, I reluctantly did what I often did when I was frustrated. I gassed up the Roadster and headed north to the Straits of Mackinac.

The northern tip of Michigan's lower peninsula resolutely juts into this treacherous aquatic blend where Lakes Michigan and Huron merge. A small village called Mackinaw City overlooks the famous narrows, providing welcome anonymity to those in need. I was in need and I knew I would not find relief in Harbor Springs.

I drove through Mackinaw City, literally to the end of the road. I had hoped to erase Kate from my mind, but I was reminded of her as I drove down the wide main street. Like Kate, Mackinaw City had an unpretentious air, an aloof attitude, and a natural beauty. I liked the city because I felt better when I was there, just as I usually did when I was with Kate. Plus it was very different from Harbor Springs, which I felt closely paralleled my parents' attributes: superficial refinement with an unemotional, cold soul

A high summer sun floated in the clear blue sky, an image that was reflected off the calm water of the Straits as I parked the Roadster outside my destination, the Keyhole Bar. I entered the bar and was enveloped by the darkness within after I closed the heavy wooden door behind me. It took a moment for my eyes to adjust. When they did I saw that the lounge was empty, save for two burly men sitting in the back by a single pool table.

I knew that despite the current calm the tavern would soon be alive with activity. The locals' long workday would end and the exhausted fudgies would retire to their motels and campsites. Then the locals' party night would begin. They always had a lot of steam to vent. The bartender, a small, compact man in his sixties, recognized me and opened an ice cold Stroh's long neck.

"Hey Joe, what's the buzz?" I said, hoisting the beer in greeting.

"Same old same old," he replied. "How's the training going?"

Joe, who retired from the Army after two World Wars, did not know me well. I was a semi-regular at best. He only knew that I came here about twice a month during the summer, drank Stroh's beer, and was reputedly a pretty good swimmer. He also assumed I was twenty-one, as he never asked for identification.

We engaged in pointless small talk until the crowd grew too large for such niceties. By this time the sun had set and I had consumed six long necks, three hard-boiled eggs, a Vienna sausage, and two bags of beer nuts. Satiated and comfortable, I shuffled to the john, stopping to place a quarter on the pool table as I passed by. I would play winner, after I peed.

The two men I saw when I had entered the Keyhole had been loudly shooting pool for the last two hours. No one dared challenge them, until me. The taller of the two, a dirty blond with a big head, appeared to be of Scandinavian descent. He sank the eight ball just as I exited the toilet and called me to the table.

"Hey fishboy, you're up," he said. I ignored the taunt, selected a stick from the wall rack and chalked my cue for the break. The man's friend was small, but muscular. He had reddish brown hair and an unkempt beard. He torqued the attack.

"I heard you talking up there at the bar, scrawn," he spat. "A skinny shit like you is in training? People tell us that you're some super swimmer. I've got a Franklin that says your full of shit. I know I can kick your ass."

"In what?" I asked calmly, "pool, or swimming? I train for swimming, but I'm here to play pool." I stepped to the table and retrieved the cue ball. "You gonna talk or rack?" I questioned the tall blond, ignoring his belligerent friend.

"I'm talking to you," the redhead interrupted. "Eric here is king of the table. After he tans your hide here I'll beat your ass in the water, stringbean. I've got a hundred dollars to back me up."

I scrutinized my muscular antagonist, this time looking at him through the eyes of a swimmer. The redhead's obvious strength didn't concern me. His swimming muscles were not well developed. His arms, neck, and legs were bulky, powerful and impressive, but too inflexible for swimming.

I had overheard them boast of their profession while shooting the bull with Joe. They were professional scuba divers, repairing the decayed pilings that threatened the North Country's many marinas. I suspected that they were strong swimmers, just not fast or flexible.

Furthermore, the redhead was visibly drunk. I was not. Plus I was at least ten years younger. I knew that he worked full-time, making him too busy to be training seriously, even if he was any good. It seemed like a good bet if the drunk was stupid enough to push it. I was certain I could beat this man in a sprint.

"You must be some swimmer," I countered strategically. "What's your name again? Where do you race?" I knew the names of most of the men in America who could potentially beat me in a sprint.

"I swim in the lake, that's where," the redhead bristled. "One hundred feet under the surface, every day. That's where. I'm a frigging sturgeon. Who the hell are you?"

"My apologies, I'm Cole Harrison. "I offered politely.

"Cole Harrison?" mocked the redhead, "I never heard of Cole Harrison. Have you Eric?"

"No way," Eric answered while pacing around the pool table, anxious for me to break.

"Hell, the way you were talking I thought maybe your name was Johnny Weissmuller," the redhead continued. "My name's McKenna, Rusty McKenna. This is Eric Nichorson. He's gonna whip you now and I'm gonna whip you later, Tarzan." I was unaffected by their bluster. I knew of no nationally ranked swimmer that was named Rusty.

"Calm down Rusty," I said nonchalantly. "If you want to swim me I say let's make it $500. I can use the money. But now let me have some fun, will you?" The tavern was now packed. Over 150 locals were crowded into the smoky saloon. The action unfolding by the pool table attracted attention, lots of attention.

"I bet you can't shoot pool any better than you can swim, Jane," Eric interjected loudly. "In fact I got a fifty that says you lose right here, right now."

"I told you, I don't bet pool," I explained patiently, "I just play for fun. You don't want to have fun; we don't have to shoot stick. It's really no big deal guys."

"Let him go Eric," Rusty said. "We'll get his jack in the water." I responded by confidently sinking the fifteen and eleven on the break. Then I ran three more stripes before Eric took his first shot.

"That's just beginner's luck," coached Rusty, "show him how a real man plays." Eric countered by sinking the six, two, one and five before missing the four by a whisper on a tough bank shot. I took advantage of the opening and cleared the table, drilling the eight ball to end the game on an even tougher bank. Without looking up, I took Rusty's quarter off the table and moved it to the coin slot.

"Looks like I saved you boys fifty dollars," I said as I turned to them. "It's your move now Rusty. Felt or water?"

"Your ass son," Rusty said, taking the challenge. "You're on: let's swim, right now, right here."

I hesitated, and then reasoned with the two men. I suggested that we race tomorrow, when Rusty wasn't drunk. This idea infuriated Rusty, who responded by snatching his quarter from me and walking towards the door.

I followed him and stopped him at the bar. I explained that I was one of the fastest swimmers around and assured him that I wasn't bragging or boasting, just stating objective, measurable fact. Rusty could not and would not beat me. This only strengthened Rusty's resolve.

Joe agreed to serve as judge. He quickly established the rules of competition as he often supervised such outrageous contests. He announced that we would race at the Mackinaw City Marina, just across the street. Then he opened the floor to bets, creating intense action.

Rusty, Eric and I left the bar. We crossed Huron Street to access the docks. After a brief search we found an acceptable course. Soon, over a 100 noisy spectators joined us, most with a piece of the action. It was almost midnight and the Keyhole was uncharacteristically empty, as were the streets of Mackinaw City.

We selected two empty slips almost directly across from each other. The total distance to be covered was about 75 yards, along a diagonal course. This appealed to me. I had an explosive start so I hoped to take an early lead. Then, after I cleared the outgoing slip I would cut to my left for about four strokes, then cut right again and sprint straight into the incoming slip. I would swim with my head buried to reduce drag. I would not look above water for landmarks. I suspected Rusty would. Such action would only slow him down.

I offered to swim in the outside lane, which Rusty accepted. I knew that even if by some miracle the race was close, I could cut Rusty off from the opposite slip. The start was the key.

I considered who would have the superior start. Racing starts are much different than scuba entry. In scuba you fall in backwards. When racing, you extend your body out and propel yourself over the water. When you enter you knife into the water and immediately streamline your body to reduce drag. Then you kick rhythmically and powerfully, which establishes your body position. Then, and only then, you begin your arm stroke. I figured that if I had a good start I would have a two body-length lead by the time I left the outbound slip.

The crowd gathered around the starting slip, positioning themselves for the best view. I left the throng for a moment to center myself. I had ten minutes, just enough time to remove all extraneous thoughts from my head. I found solitude a few slips down. I sat on the end of an empty dock, sandwiched between two sailboats. I heard only the water gently lapping against the pier and the bottoms of the boats. I visualized my swim. Soon I was ready. These boys would pay for their ignorance.

Then moments later, it was over. As planned, I had a great start. I cut sharply left once clear of the outgoing slip and drew well ahead of Rusty, who held his head high above the water. He saw me ahead of him and buried his head briefly to dig deep and strong. When he looked up again, five strokes later, I had made my second cut and was close to the finish. The enthusiastic crowd had cheered me on. Rusty was still in the main channel when I finished. The race had not even been close.

I collected my winnings and the crowd escorted me back to the Keyhole where they heralded my achievement. Celebrating my win, they boisterously toasted me for the rest of night. Finally I left. As I got into the Roadster I looked at the early morning silhouette of the marina, brightened by a faint pre-dawn glow. A broad smile filled my face. The North Country had delivered. Kate was not on my mind.

Chapter Five

WAXING QUARTER

Monday, July 3

AUPETCHI

Sawmay was certain that Audawmeg's spirit had come to me, through Kate. He said Audawmeg's message was clear: Odawgen must do everything possible to meet the needs of the Anabe. It is why Odawgen existed. If racing could advance the needs of the people, then Aupetchi must race. It was Odawgen's duty, his responsibility. So, secure in our ancestor's blessing, Sawmay quickly developed a strategy.

The barriers to my success were as obvious as the goal. I must win, but how? Odawgen had never raced. Not that competition was infrequent among us; we loved sport. It was just done on dry land, except for an occasional canoe race. Odawgen filled a spiritual role and we feared that competition could stain his sanctity.

Sawmay reminded me that the *waubesh* did not often honor tradition, did not embrace ritual. Cole would not defer to, or even acknowledge, Odawgen's sanctity. In fact, if Cole was among the worst of the *waubesh*, he might even welcome the opportunity to humiliate the Anabe by defeating Odawgen. I suspected that Cole was among the worst. Maymegwan often complained about Cole in my presence. It displeased her, as it did me, that Kate loved this insolent boy. Maymegwan called him a man without character.

But Maymegwan also knew he shared my passion for swimming, and that he knew how to race. She told me that Cole was trying to become the world's fastest swimmer. She said he trained for many hours, every day, and had done so for many years. When I shared this knowledge with Sawmay, he grew more concerned. He directed me to train more diligently.

The wise man knew that I only swam a few days a week, at best, and even this only during the warm weather moons. Odawgen's swim required endurance, not speed. In fact, the slower I went, the better. The longer it took me to complete my ritual swim, the more frenzied the crowd was when I arrived. This encouraged me to swim at a steady, slow pace. I did this very well. After considering these facts, Sawmay concluded that I needed a drastic change. I agreed.

I could not win if I swam as Odawgen did. I had to learn to swim like Cole. We decided that I must leave Tawkenin and train for many hours for many days. When not swimming I would meditate and visualize victory. I could no longer see swimming as ritual; I needed to see it as war. I had to focus solely on Odawgen's ultimate mission: to prepare for and win this race, and in the process, somehow save Tawkenin. To facilitate this, Sawmay ordered me to travel north. It was the only way. So, two days after running into Kate at Bliss Beach, I joined a small entourage that quietly departed Tawkenin in two long birch canoes. We headed north.

It rained as we paddled up the coast so we stayed close to the foggy shore. That way, safe harbor remained accessible if needed. Finally we beached, two days after departing. I disembarked and watched as the canoes left me alone. After they faded into the mist I scouted my location, a place I had often heard of but never seen.

By early evening I was sitting in front of a warm fire roasting my dinner, my small permanent camp positioned behind me. I stirred the embers before rising to look about. The sun sat low on the horizon. The two-day rain had stopped, and the sky was clear. The air was humid and calm, the lake motionless.

My camp sat on a seemingly insignificant peninsula with two small islands offshore. I stood facing the Inland Sea. Behind me the peninsula disappeared into a thick cedar forest, the white bark of scattered birches tempering the darkness of the dense interior. Smooth, round stones littered the small beach I camped upon. Most were black, gray or white; many gleamed with vibrant shades of red, blue, green, and countless variations thereof. I gathered two twisted pieces of driftwood. One served as a table, the other as a backrest. I positioned them by the fire, then returned to the tip of the tiny peninsula. I looked back to my fire.

Although the peninsula was insignificant, it was not inconsequential. My people, the Anabe, revered it. We called it Waugoshance. As I faced my camp I admired the forest that served as the beaches eastern border. I listened intently as Michi Gama lapped against the small peninsula's southern shore. Behind me, the sun slipped into twilight. To the north, the fabled Straits of Mackinac began. I would train where the waters met.

The fire crackled loudly, interrupting my rumination, so I returned to tend to it. After calming the flame I sat and thought of my sister Maymegwan. She was among the crew who had traveled here with me. They would return for me only when I was ready. Meanwhile, Maymegwan continued on with them, because she had business to attend to up north. She was going to trade with the *waubesh* in Mackinaw City.

Our grandmother taught Maymegwan to craft exquisite jewelry out of porcupine quills, just as her grandmother had taught her. Maymegwan made earrings mostly, and there was a great demand for her creations in Mackinaw City. Initially, May only sold her work at our Pow Wow. In time she learned that her handiwork would sell well elsewhere. She discussed this opportunity with our family, and after a time they agreed. She chose Mackinaw City as her outlet.

They agreed because they felt May would be continuing a long tribal tradition. The region had always been a major trading center - even before the Europeans arrived. The Anabe formed strong trade alliances with many Native nations. We met at the end of each summer on the south shore of the Straits. In fact that is where we were when the French arrived. They constructed a fortified trading post there, on the north shore. They named the post St. Ignace. After many successful years they moved the post to the southern shore and renamed it Michilimackinac. Eventually the French surrendered this post to

the British who started the settlement that became
Mackinaw City. Then the British moved the post one final
time, to Mackinac Island where the United States flag
first flew.

The Anabe were always among the most successful
traders, regardless of the location or national allegiance of
the post. Consequently, our family felt it was Maymegwan's destiny to sell her creations in this region, albeit to
a few select stores.

Mackinaw City offered many "native crafts" but few of
them were genuine and none as beautiful as Maymegwan's. She had paddled her first inventory ashore just
over a year ago and it had sold well, very well. She made
five more trips to Mackinaw by canoe before the autumn
winds prohibited lake travel. Nine men accompanied her,
in a canoe similar to those used by the French voyageurs.
It held up to ten adults and three hundred pounds of
cargo. On this trip my supplies made up the bulk of the
cargo, which was fine since May's creations were light and
compact.

I was happy she pursued this. Anything she did that
embraced Anabe tradition pleased me. I was concerned at
times because she seemed content to abandon many of our
time-honored ways. The most obvious was her decision to
attend the local school. She developed some habits there
that I did not approve of, like her manner of dress. I protested, but she said she had to wear *waubesh* clothes to
school so she wouldn't "stick out" and be ridiculed even
more than she already was. However, when she traveled
to Mackinaw City she dressed in the Anabe manner,
which made my support of this effort even stronger.

She had left me three days ago. Since then I had established a routine. Each morning I swam from the
western tip of the peninsula to and around an island we
knew as Kezhekekee. Then I would cross the open lake to
the island the area was named after, Waugoshance. There
I would rest briefly, forage for some fresh berries, and
then swim back.

Shifting sandbars and massive rock outcroppings sat in the waters, making the lake more turbulent than I had expected. My swim took more than seven hours the first day. Fortunately, my time improved with every effort I kept finding an easier path through the water, like marking a trail in the forest. I developed an easy rhythm that let me synchronize my breathing with the rise and fall of each swell. As the water rose I kicked powerfully and stretched my long arms into the mountain of water. At the peak I exhaled through my nose while pulling furiously with short, deep arm strokes. I relaxed my kick just a bit, then sprinted down the descending swell. At the low point I inhaled and started the cycle once again.

Today it took me less than six hours to complete the swim. I was quickly becoming one with the water. This had been a very good day, my best day so far. I returned to camp and feasted upon fresh sturgeon and dried venison. I thanked Manitou a bit more devoutly than usual. Satiated and satisfied, I laid down under a bright, clear sky. The stars above comforted me as I drifted to sleep. Once there, I inexplicably dreamt I was battling a scorpion.

COLE

I started my day with a 5,000-yard workout. First I swam a long warm-up, and then some slow distance swims with short rest intervals. To close practice, Olivia threw in some starts and turns. She knew how to keep things interesting. Still I was distracted during the workout, which concerned my sister.

"Cole, you swam great. You're really beginning to develop a good sense of pace," Olivia suggested, hoping to encourage me.

"Yeah sure," I replied without conviction.

"Cole Harrison," she said authoritatively stopping me in my tracks, "what is wrong with you? You should be feeling great right now. I've never seen you train so well. Why aren't you happy?"

"Look sis, I'm sorry. It's not the swimming. You're doing a great job. Really, I feel like I can beat the world right now," I answered.

"Maybe," she replied, "but only if your head is in the swim. Right now it's not and I want to know why."

I sat on a starting block and finished drying myself. Olivia handed me a sweatshirt, which I pulled on.

"It's Kate," I told her. "I just never know what kind of mood she's going to be in. Some days she's eager to see me, but other days - it seems like most days, lately - she just wants to be left alone. I don't get it."

Olivia sat on the concrete deck, facing me. She wrapped her arms around her legs and pulled them to her chest. She spoke to me as a sister, not as a coach.

"Cole, you know how hard Kate works. You've been to the White Pine. Everyone says that the Kilpatrick women run the best restaurant in town. That's hard work, real hard work, and not just physically but mentally, too. They have to put up with a lot of bull," she reasoned. "Maybe she's just tired."

"I've thought of that. I know she's tired and I understand that they work hard, but no harder than they have the last two summers. And she saw me a lot more then. There's got to be more to it than work," I argued.

Olivia agreed with this logic. It made sense and she understood why.

"Do you remember Douglas Hayes?" she asked.

"Of course, you broke up with him three years ago," I answered. "He was like one of the family before that."

"And do you know why we broke up?" she continued.

"No, I just figured it was because he graduated," I said.

"That was part of it," she explained, "but there was more to it. The thing is, when you see someone for as long as I saw Douglas, and for as long as you've seen Kate, you get to a crossroads. At least, women get to a crossroads."

"What do you mean?" I asked curiously.

"I mean you and Kate have been dating for three summers now. Do you do anything different than you did three years ago?" she asked.

"Not really. We just drive around, hang out, go out to eat, or to beach parties. Same stuff," I answered.

"Exactly," she said. "That's just how Douglas was. Everything was fine as long as it stayed the same. The problem was, I didn't want things to stay the same and I bet Kate doesn't either."

"Then what does she want? What did you want?"

"I wanted to grow and I wanted the relationship to mature," she explained. "I bet Kate wants to know where your relationship is headed."

I ran a towel through my hair and thought for a moment.

"She doesn't want marriage, does she?" I finally asked.

"Well, that's close. I think what she really wants is a sense of commitment. She wants to know where you two are going," Olivia suggested.

The pool office telephone rang. I answered it, interrupting our discussion. It was Kate. She told me she would get off work at six and hoped she could see me. My mood suddenly improved.

"Thanks sis," I called to Olivia, "that helped. I'll get my brain in the game, I promise."

Then I retired to the locker room, impatient for the evening to arrive. Despite my growing concern I was eager to see Kate.

◆◆◆

Later that night I picked her up at the White Pine, and realized exactly how much I missed her. I longed to hold her close but knew better than to rush into it. I would give her some space and let her get comfortable with my presence. Then I would act.

We headed north to Mackinaw City. The Roadster was quickly filled with her sweet, perfumed aroma. The scent of her freshly shampooed hair induced a sense of comfort in me I had long forgotten. My serenity increased as Harbor Springs faded from my rearview mirror.

Harbor Springs was old money personified. Indulgent shops filled her streets. In them, one could find fashion, art, and cuisine right off the streets of Manhattan. Moored in her marina were expensive yachts from such ports as Del Ray Beach, Gross Pointe Shores, Lake Forest, and Miami Beach. Exclusive resorts, like Harbor Point and Wequetonsing, were with in her city limits.

The broad streets of Mackinaw City were quite different. Unlike Harbor Springs, Mackinaw City was rarely a final destination. Instead it was the last stop on the road to Michigan's Upper Peninsula. Mackinaw City housed massive ferries that carried tens of thousands of cars to the Upper Peninsula each summer. Despite having the broadest street north of Detroit, some five lanes wide, visitors rarely stayed long. Instead they restocked their coolers and quickly got in line, waiting to board a coal-fired ferry.

Nearby Mackinac Island was also accessible by ferry from the City, but a single lane handled the traffic it generated. These ferries carried only passengers since the island had banned automobiles in 1901. Island travel was done by foot, horse, or bicycle, which deterred the advance purchase of supplies in Mackinaw City.

The City's commerce mirrored her status as a layover. Party stores, fudge shops, grocery stores, bait shops, diners and bars filled her streets. The notable exception was a unique shop featuring shipwreck merchandise. It sold salvaged items recovered from the many victims of the treacherous Straits of Mackinac. Kate had told me this was one of the shops where her friend May sold jewelry.

Yachts did not sit in Mackinaw City's marina. Instead, fishing boats from places like Cheyboygan, Rogers City, and Alpena filled her slips. The Straits, where Lake Huron and Lake Michigan meet, were as fertile with fish as they were dangerous to ships.

We arrived in Mackinaw City an hour later, refreshed from our leisurely drive. I found a prime parking space on Mackinaw City's broad Central Street. We crossed through the ferry traffic to hit our first stop - the Keyhole, of course. Joe welcomed me like a hero.

"Here he is folks," Joe announced, "the fastest swimmer in Mackinaw, Keyhole's Cole Harrison. And who is this beautiful lady?"

"Thanks Joe. Now I'm totally embarrassed," I replied. "Have you seen those two rubes again?"

"Not since you three wandered out that night. I think their pride hurt as much as their hangover when they woke up the next morning," Joe said. "No big loss though. They were more trouble than they were worth. Now who's your lady?"

"Oh sorry, Joe. This is Kate, from Harbor Springs," I said.

"Woo hoo," Joe replied mockingly, "Harbor Springs is it? Then I spoke correctly, she really is a lady. Good catch Cole."

Joe did not know that it was actually I who had all the money. I was protective of my identity in Mackinaw.

"It's not like that Joe," I countered. "Kate works there with her mother Helen, at the White Pine Inn."

"Helen, as in Helen Kilpatrick?" asked Joe.

"That's right. Do you know her?" I answered.

"I know of her, that's for sure. She's a legend in this business. And you're her daughter Kate. I've heard a lot about you too - they say you're even better than Helen is," Joe asserted.

It was Kate's turn to blush. Joe's praise caught her off guard and the mention of her mother's name had alerted her defenses. She was certain Joe would now comment on one of Helen's idiosyncrasies. He did not.

"Why thank you Joe," she finally said, "it's nice of you to say that."

"Hey, people in the biz have to stick together you know," Joe explained with a wink.

The three of us huddled together for an hour as the crowd filtered in. Joe and Kate traded war stories while I offered what I could, when I could. I drank a few bottles of Stroh's and Kate sipped a glass of Coca-Cola. When Joe's rush was about to begin Kate and I left to find another oasis.

We detoured up Henry Street, crossed Etherington and Jamet, and cut across the parking lot of the Church of the Straits. We jogged across Huron Street past the large ferry dock that housed the coal-burning icebreaker, *Chief Wawatam.*

"Cole, let's take all this in. This is beautiful and I never get up here in the summer. I'm always too busy," Kate said as she took my hand in hers.

It was indeed a beautiful evening. The sun was just beginning to set and the huge Michigan sky was alive with color. Kate led me to a small service dock jutting into the Straits. To our right was Lake Huron, where the sky was already gray and dark. To our left was Lake Michigan, where the sun was setting brilliantly. Directly in front of us, across the Straits was the Upper Peninsula shoreline. A cool northwest breeze drove the day's heat and humidity away. The night's first lonely stars appeared above us.

"Why don't we just stay here all night, Cole? There's a blanket in the car and a party store right down the street," Kate suggested.

She drew my hand to her heart; I could feel it beating beneath her thin cotton shirt. I noticed it was beating rapidly.

"Kate, I miss you so much," I said as I kissed her forehead.

She buried her head into my chest and I wrapped my arms around her. In the distance the sound of a foghorn bellowed, followed by the blasts of ship's whistle as it navigated the Straits. Between these calls we could hear only gentle waves lapping at the shore. Kate looked to me.

"What are you thinking?" I asked.

"About my father," she said. "He's lost somewhere out there, you know, in that vast expanse."

I tightened the grip of my arms around her, hoping it would comfort her.

"As I watch that ship I know that somewhere, sometime, another little girl will lose her daddy," she murmured as she began to tear lightly.

I slowly slipped my right hand under her blouse and caressed the small of her back. Finding no resistance I slowly worked my left hand under her shirt and moved towards her breasts. Kate stiffened suddenly.

"What's wrong Kate? I thought you wanted to cuddle here."

"That's right Cole, cuddle, not neck. It's been so long since we've been together I want to feel you near me again first."

The freighter playing Marco Polo with the foghorn passed directly in front of us. Like most mariners' children, Kate knew her ships well.

"She's the *Cedarville*," Kate said, trying to change the subject. "Isn't she beautiful?"

"Not as beautiful as you Kate." Cole leaned back a bit, thoughtfully. "You know it's actually a lot like me. Big, long, and deep. Now what's it going to be, necking or Clinkers?"

"Gee Cole, when you're so understanding and roman-tic you leave me no choice. Clinkers it is."

Kate rolled her eyes as she broke my embrace and left the park. She did not react as I ran to catch up to her. In-stead she stopped, let me pass, and watched the freighter move slowly through the Straits.

"Safe voyage," she whispered before turning back to me.

We linked arms and walked slowly down Huron Street, following the shoreline. We were headed for the Clinker's Club.

KATE

I liked Clinker's because it was more of dance hall than a tavern. Cole liked the Keyhole for exactly the opposite reason. Both served food, which is why we could get in despite being under twenty-one years old. And neither ever carded Cole, which is why he liked Mackinaw City. It didn't matter to me, since I didn't drink much. Only when Cole brought beer along on our evening drives or at a beach party would I sip a little. And it's not like Cole was a heavy drinker, he wasn't. He took his training seriously. But he did like beer, and he liked the camaraderie he found when enjoying a bottle or two. So it was fine with me when we went to Mackinaw City. I knew Cole needed a night out now and then, and it was good for him to get away from Harbor Springs and the family legend that followed him there.

This had been a long night. It was after midnight when we left Clinker's, and my spirits were high. Cole had been attentive to me and was particularly interested in my work, which was unusual. Instead of leaving me alone for much of the evening while he played pool, he led me to a relatively private booth where we talked and laughed between dances like the friends we were. Then, when Clinker's closed we walked north along the shoreline, slowly returning to the Roadster. A tiny tip of the waxing moon began to rise from the lake.

"They're all out now hon," I said to Cole, looking up.

"Who's out Kate?" he replied, looking around. "It seems pretty desolate to me."

His observation was accurate. The streets of Mackinaw City were empty.

"The stars, Cole, the stars," I answered. "They're all out. Look."

Cole looked to the sky and saw that the heavens were indeed alive with activity. The remote night sky of the far north revealed a crystal clear panorama. The motel and tourist trap lights were now dark, and moonlight was not yet a factor. Cole marveled at the celestial illumination. The view above him literally stopped him in his tracks.

"Wow," he exclaimed. "That's something. They're everywhere."

"That they are. It's another thing I love about Mackinaw. Do you see those three bright stars?" I said as I outlined a triangle high above us.

"No, I don't," Cole said. "Wait, which ones are they?"

"The brightest of the bright," I explained while patiently pointing each out separately. "That one is called Altar. That one over there is Deneb. The third is Vega. They're called the summer triangle. They are the brightest summer stars, so we see them first every evening. They're the stars we saw when we were at the park earlier, before dusk."

"Oh yeah. They were out then," Cole reflected. "Cool stuff, Kate. How do you know that? Your not getting smart on me now, are you?" he teased.

"Getting and got, babe. My father taught me when I was just a girl," I said before pausing to treasure my father's memory. "Whenever he came ashore in the summer my father always took me to the beach by our house."

Cole sensed he should not rush this narrative and remained silent. I continued, deliberately.

"His favorite time to take me was at night. He said that's what he loved best about working the lakes - the evenings on the open water," I explained. "He said that stars were brilliant, unimaginably plentiful, and seemed to be unusually close to the water out there. Sometimes he felt like he could reach out and gather them in."

Cole considered my comments for moment.

"That's really sweet, Kate. He sounds like a great guy. I wish I could have known him," he said. "Tell me, do you still miss him?"

Cole's empathy silenced me. His interest stunned me. He rarely inquired about my family. He had never even asked to see my beach, even though I spoke of it often. He had certainly never spoken to me about my father.

"Every day," I replied honestly, "I miss him every single day. So many things remind me of him: the beach, the lake, the sounds of the freighters passing. I even see bits of him in some of the people I meet. It seems like every day I recognize some movement of his in a customer, or see part of his personality in someone I know."

Cole paused again to contemplate my remarks. Then he continued, tentatively.

"Do you ever see parts if him in me?" he asked.

Once more, this caught me off guard. This was a strange and wonderfully welcome Cole. He was interested in my feelings and sensitive to my needs. After some private reflection I decided to reveal a thin layer of my soul to him.

I had never told him so, but Cole did remind me of my father. For one thing, neither my father and nor Cole had delivered what I desired from them. I prayed for my father to return home unharmed and I longed for Cole to be my husband someday. Both outcomes seemed equally hopeless.

Plus, Cole was a long way from being the type of man I hoped to marry; yet I optimistically believed that someday he would be. I knew in my heart that Cole had it in him, whatever "it" was. I wasn't one to bother with details when it came to love. I would know "it" when I saw it.

"Kind of," I finally answered. "You're both Scorpio's."

"Really? Like astrology, right? When was his birthday?"

"Eight days after yours, November 16," I said. "Would you like to see your constellation? It's out now."

"Sure, but you mean our constellation, don't you? Your fathers and mine."

I moved close to him and wrapped one arm around his waist.

"That's right, your constellation, Stan and Cole's," I agreed. "There it is now, rising in the western sky."

"Really, you can see it? I always thought of astrology

as fiction. More myths from the dark ages," he said doubt-
fully. "You're just full of hidden talents tonight, Kate."

"Oh they're not so hidden, Cole. You've just never
looked before," I chided.

"You may be right about that," he admitted.

I forged ahead.

"In any case of course you can see them. Astrology is
based on the constellations. Your zodiac sign is the most
influential constellation when you're born," I explained,
cherishing this special time together. "I know it because
my father told me so. He'd bring me out here with a
thermos of hot chocolate, tiny marshmallows, and some
meat pasties. We'd have a "midnight picnic" under the
stars. He'd point out Scorpio and explain how Scorpio
cleared the way for Sagittarius, my sign. He told me that
just like the stars, he would clear danger out of my way."

"So December is Sagittarius?" Cole asked.

"Well, December 12 is. It really depends on the date.
Some of December is Scorpio, too," I explained. "Anyhow,
do you recognize the Milky Way?"

"Sure I do," Cole said with some pride. "It's that long,
kind of fluffy streak running across the sky. Olivia
showed it to me."

"That's right. Good for Olivia. Now follow the Milky
Way to the western horizon," I said, leading his vision
with my right arm. "Find the group of stars just above the
tree line that looks like a little teapot, short and stout."

"As in 'here is my handle, here is my spout.' I got it
Kate. Which one is that?"

"That's me, Sagittarius," I said.

"Oh, that's not you honey. You're much better looking," he joked, and then instinctively moved closer to me.

"Cole, you scoundrel," I blushed. "Now, look to the
right of the teapot until you see a bright red star. It's in
the middle of what looks like a sideways T."

"A red star eh? Cool! I see it!" he exclaimed excitedly.

"Good. That's Antares. The inverted T is the main
section of Scorpio, which is a giant scorpion. The T is its

body. My father told me that Antares is the scorpion's heart and that's why it's red," I explained.

"Awesome Kate. I always wanted to see my big red heart," he said absent-mindedly.

"And to think it was right above you all along," I added, sharing his amazement.

Later, emotionally content and comfortably entwined we slowly returned to the car. I relaxed in the big leather seat as the Roadster left Mackinaw City. I realized that my affection for Cole had grown; he was beginning to develop the maturity and sensitivity I had hoped for since I first laid eyes on him.

I felt his love completely when we stopped at the deserted Mackinaw City Municipal Beach, five miles west of the City. Cole had packed a twelve-pack of Stroh's in the trunk as usual. This time though, instead of removing the beer he reached past it, deep into the cavernous trunk, and removed a hidden blanket.

"Okay Kate, how about those cuddles we talked about?" he asked.

I smiled as we interlocked arms once again and traipsed to the beach. We quickly found a secluded hollow behind a dune. Cole laid out the blanket and took me in his arms. He held me close, protectively, and then pulled me to the soft sand bed.

"Rest easy sweetness," Cole whispered in my ear. "Your scorpion is here and no danger will find you."

Then he held me tightly - just held me. He did not force himself upon me. He did not initiate intimacy. He did not speak. Comforted and astonished, I quickly fell asleep. Warmed by Cole's broad swimmers shoulders and cradled in his long, well-toned arms I slept deeply. I dreamt of my father Stanley Kilpatrick. In my dream he had finally returned to Bliss. After many years of searching, all was well in my world.

Chapter Six

WANING QUARTER

Tuesday, July 18

COLE

What I remember first about this morning was the humidity. By eight a.m. the air temperature had already reached 82 degrees, and the humidity was over 80%. I broke into a sweat just approaching the pool for my morning workout. I tentatively dipped my right foot into the water, which felt much cooler than the air. The thermometer said it was 78 degrees, but it felt icy. I leaned over and palmed the water with my right, then my left hand and gently tempered each shoulder. Then I cupped the water with both hands and immersed my face. This process took a full three minutes. Finally, I elongated into a full body stretch and stared intently at the pool, oblivious of my sister Olivia waiting patiently beside me. Exasperated, she urged me on.

"Come on, Cole. The sooner you start, the sooner we'll finish," she said, emphasizing the "we."

"All right already," I replied, holding my focus. Then I broke concentration and relaxed my muscles. I backed away from the edge of the pool. "I don't understand it, Olivia, I've swum nearly every day of my life for the past ten years and I still hate getting into the pool."

"I know you do Cole," she agreed, " and that's because you think about it too much. Just go to the edge of the pool and jump in. It's simple."

"To you maybe, but not for me," I argued. "I have to get psyched up first."

"So get psyched little brother," she instructed. "I'll be quiet. Just hurry if you can. I need to talk to you after practice so GET GOING!"

And so I did. Two hours and 4,050 yards later I was done. I finished my workout as I always did, with five full deep water bobs.

Olivia handed me a towel and held my T-shirt while I dried myself. The shirt was gray with royal blue lettering. It read, *Bay City Central Swimming*, my less-than-subtle dig at the elitist Harrison family history. My father, Four, rarely mentioned the city where One rose to greatness, because Two crashed in failure there. My derision did not amuse Four, but he tolerated it. My mother Elizabeth told me I was inconsiderate. Neither parent understood me, but both seemed to admire my spirit. They wisely avoided corralling it. I suspect they both hoped I would rein it in eventually. Olivia spoke again.

"Great job Cole. You're so primed," she said.

"Thanks to you," I acknowledged.

She gave me the T-shirt, which I haphazardly pulled on. It seemed to read *Baty Swing*.

"Now what's up?" I asked.

"Do you remember when you told me about your race in the Mackinaw City Marina?" she inquired.

"I do. That felt so right. I was unbeatable," I beamed. "I think even Kate is starting to notice how well I'm swimming."

"Exactly my point," Olivia replied. "I want to tap into that attitude and see if you can use it in the pool."

"How do you mean?" I asked as I straightened my shirt. *Bay City Central Swimming* was finally legible.

"Well, it's like this. You're talented enough to make the Olympics. Your technique is flawless and your endurance is strong. But you need to develop a sense of pace."

"Like yours?" I asked. "I though that was a natural gift."

"For some it is, but not for me. I had to work on it, develop it. It took a lot of effort," Olivia confirmed.

Olivia possessed a strong sense of pace. This ability allowed her to mentally break each race into small segments. She could calculate the speed she needed to maintain for each 25-yard lap of a race in order to achieve her desired time. Then she could go out and do it, physically.

I could do it in practice, but not in meets. The adrenaline overwhelmed me. My splits would be all over the place when I raced for distance. Olivia knew that this range in splits increased my potential for error. She had seen too many swimmers who took 200's out too fast, making them overly tired for the finish. In extreme cases they swam much slower than anticipated, which killed their chances in the race. Natural pacers like Olivia swam consistently, so their times were steady.

The contrasting strategies often created exciting races. When swimming against people of equal talent, a good pacer could be two or three body lengths behind the leader after the first 100 yards and still catch and pass them during the second. This was a common occurrence during Olivia's career.

Since I swam the 60 and 100 yard Freestyle in prep school, I never had to pace myself. The 60 was an all-out sprint and the 100 utilized minimal pace. My sense of pace was seldom tested, which was what worried Olivia.

"You need to get some distance race experience before you go to Michigan State. College swimming is very different from prep school swimming. It will help you. Plus, I think your best chance for the Olympics is in the 4x200 Free Relay."

"Well I am swimming across Little Traverse Bay this summer. Doesn't that count as experience?"

"It helps for sure, but you need more than one race."

"All right then, you're the coach. I'll race some distance. But I can still try out for the 100 Free, can't I?" I asked.

"Of course you can, and will. You should also enter the 400 Freestyle. It will help both your 100 and the relay. The 400 depends on your sense of pace and you can get some experience in strategy events," Olivia explained.

"Yea, that sounds good. I need some new trophies," I boasted.

"Don't get ahead of yourself, Cole. This will be against some tough competition. Your days of glaring down high school boys are over. The Olympics means well-trained men who know all the psyche trips," Olivia cautioned.

"You're right, of course, Olivia. So when do we start?"

"In a few weeks. We're going back to Detroit early, before the end of the summer."

"Not during the summer! It's too hot and humid downstate. Isn't that why we leave?" I pleaded.

"It's only for the weekend," she assured me. "The Water Wonderland has an open division. It draws American college swimmers from as far away as California. Sometimes the Australians come too."

"I know, I remember. I finaled in the Junior 50 and you won the Open 200 Backstroke two years ago," I recalled.

"That we did little brother," she said while leading me away from the pool.

◆◆◆

Two and a half hours later we joined our parents for lunch in the summer cottage's grand formal dining room. Olivia and I arrived late. Our dress was too casual for our parents' taste; consequently, a bothersome silence filled the room when we entered. We sat before a pre-set cup of cold *vichyssoise*, served on a china saucer with a French lace underliner. Olivia devoured her *potage* while I avoided mine.

Bradford cleared both cups when Olivia finished, then returned with a freshly tossed Caesar salad. I had always loved this course: aged grated Italian Parmesan cheese, imported Sicilian anchovies, fresh California spinach, and crumbled bacon from freshly butchered Michigan pork. A platter of fresh baked cherry-nut roll was placed on the table, still warm from the oven. They featured Traverse City cherries, harvested some eighty miles southwest. Freshly churned local butter accompanied them.

Bradford the butler then appeared with a bottle of Dom Perignon and an ice bucket

"Your father told me this was a special occasion for you. Congratulations," he said as he filled the crystal champagne glasses.

"Really. Is that so father? I didn't know," I asked while gulping a fortifying sip of the bubbly.

"And how could you? I've had no time to tell you. You've missed dinner three times this week," Four replied.

I unwittingly flinched at the subtle reprimand.

"I am sorry father. Olivia's been working me pretty hard."

"Indeed she has Cole, thankfully. She tells me you've never swum better," Four replied.

"Absolutely!" Olivia confirmed. "He's smooth in the water."

"She also tells us that you're certain to qualify for the Olympics. We are all so proud," my mother added.

"Now I never said certain. I said he certainly had a chance," Olivia corrected.

"Thank you mother," I replied modestly, ignoring Olivia's implication, "I hope I will fulfill your wishes."

"Oh you will son, you will," Four interjected, "and to that end I got some good news from the bank today."

"Really sir? Did another stock split?"

"Well, not that good, but good enough. Especially for you," Four said.

"I'm interested," I replied.

"Me too. So let's cut to the chase. What's up?" Olivia asked.

"Last week I exercised an option on some prime real estate. Cole Harrison was granted full title to over ten thousand acres of God's country."

"Great for you father, really," I answered absently, not really listening.

"Cole, did you hear what father said?" asked Olivia.

"Sure I did. He got some more real estate. I congratulated him," I answered defensively.

"No, he said Cole Harrison got some land. That's you silly," she explained. "He's giving YOU the Indian land up north."

"It's not Indian land, Olivia. They have no claim to title," father interjected.

"Actually, that's not entirely true, father. Kate told me a lot about it. She says the Anishinabe claimed title back when the French were here," I offered.

"Really? That's interesting," Olivia mused. "I never knew that."

"That's because no claim has been ever been produced. French, English, American or Indian," Four said conclusively.

"Are you sure?" I asked.

"I'm sure. We couldn't get title if they had," Four answered.

"I'll have to ask Kate again. I must have heard her wrong."

"See what I mean about concentration and focus, little brother?" Olivia teased. "You can't keep up and you can't get things straight."

"Okay, okay. I give," I feigned surrender to my sister, then turned to father: "This is too generous sir. You said I was going to manage a development for you, work my way up."

"You will. It's just that after what Olivia tells me, I'm sure the Olympic gold medal will be yours. It won't look right if I have you managing the development. People will think I don't have confidence in your ability. You need to own it too," Four explained.

After lunch, Olivia and I excused ourselves and escaped to the dock with half-filled glasses of Dom. Four and Elizabeth watched us absently from the porch of the massive cottage, no doubt wondering what we children were saying to each other.

"That's a pretty cool gift Cole," Olivia said tentatively. "Can I live there too?"

"You can build right next to me," I assured her.

We turned to watch an eclectic flotilla of boats sailing on Little Traverse Bay.

"So," Olivia said after a long moment, "why are you so glum?"

"Didn't you hear him?" I lamented. "Even when he

gives me something he insults me. I'm just another tro-
phy. The land is just a bigger pedestal for them to display
me on. That's all."

"I don't agree Cole. If it's your land, you can do what
you want. He can only control what you do if you let him,"
she reasoned.

"I just wish I could do something to show him that I
was my own man. That I had a mind, and a plan, of my
own," I countered. "Maybe I'll quit swimming. That would
ruin his plans."

"No way! You love to swim. You can't stop doing something that brings you pleasure. You'd hurt yourself more
than him," she reasoned. "If you do anything to make 'a
statement' of independence it should bring you pleasure."

I thought about what she said and it made sense.
What could I do that would bring me pleasure, and make
Four miserable? There had to be something.

Olivia placed her arm around me as I continued to
brood. We sat together in silence for a long while. Then I
slapped her on the knee and said, "That does it then. I
have to go run an errand. It's time to do something for
me."

KATE

Cole arrived at the White Pine Inn late that evening, after my double shift ended. He was upbeat and positive. He had called me ahead of time to tell two things: The first was to dress formally, which I managed to do only after my mother ran downtown and bought me a new dress. The second was to tell me about his father's seemingly generous gift. It was one thing for him to sell homes for his father, it was quite another to for him to sell homes for himself. Cole said the undeveloped land alone was worth up to a half a million dollars. When developed it would be worth more, maybe ten times more. His future, and possibly our future, had become secure.

Anyway, I knew something else was up when he came to get me. He parked in front of the main entrance to the Inn, which was unusual. Mom insisted that all employees use the rear service dock, and that meant anyone picking up an employee, even - no make that especially - her daughter. And if that wasn't bold enough, he was wearing a black tuxedo complete with cummerbund, cane, and top hat. I was a little embarrassed and very excited when we left the Inn and climbed into the Buick. I was grateful he called ahead and asked me to "dress formally."

"Your chariot awaits, M'lady," Cole said as he held the door open for me.

He bowed deeply as I entered and sat down. I turned my blushing face and looked to the front window of the Inn. Mom smiled to me and waved in encouragement, despite her frustration with Cole's incessant irreverence. After Cole got in, I turned to him.

"What's gotten into you?" I whispered.

He said nothing; instead he reached behind me and produced the biggest bouquet of roses and carnations I had ever seen.

"Love, my dear. Love, hope and happiness, that's what's gotten into me."

"Well, may God bless love, hope and happiness then.

These are absolutely beautiful. Thank you," I gushed while smelling the bouquet.

"And still their beauty pales when held in your arms," Cole cooed.

Then he pulled away from the White Pine Inn, guiding the Roadster down Bay Street and onto Pennsylvania Avenue. Then he turned right on Artesian and drove west along Beach Drive.

"So what in the world is going on, Cole? Is this about the land, or did you beat some more divers at the marina?" I teased.

"Better than either my sweet," he said mysteriously, "better than either."

This relieved me for a moment; after our talk earlier, I had been troubled about his land gift. I had reviewed in my mind where he said it was and it seemed to me that it included Tawkenin, where my best friend and the Anabe people lived. Again, I pushed this thought from my mind, I wanted to enjoy this moment as best I could.

Cole drove past Wequetonsing and pulled into the parking lot of Harbor Springs' most formal restaurant, Chez Robert. He opened my door, helped me out of the car and led me into the dining room. After being seated at a secluded lakefront table, Cole handed my flowers to the *maitre' D.*

"Place those in water, my good man, and bring us a bottle of your best sparkling water," directed Cole.

"Cole Harrison, tell me what in the world is going on," I demanded.

"After we get the bubbly my dear," Cole replied.

A white-coated waiter with a stiff black bow tie appeared and poured the sparkling water into champagne glasses, icing the bottle before leaving us in solitude. Just to be sure about things I asked him again where this land was that his father had given him. He told me.

"You mean he has given you full title to Tawkenin?" I asked.

"I guess so Kate. But Olivia and I both asked Four

about that, and he said that your friends don't have a legal claim to it."

"Really? I'll have to ask May about that," I said, temporarily relieved.

Maybe it was all on the up and up.

"It does seem a bit out of character for Four, though.
He's really letting go of the old puppet strings," I answered.

"Oh, he was in full character. Don't worry about that.
The only reason he gave it to me is so he would look wise,
not because he has any confidence in my business sense.
He just thinks it would look tacky to give it to me after
the Olympics," Cole explained as he refilled our glasses.

"Hmmm, old dog, old tricks. Imagine that," I mused.
"Well it will take some of the pressure off of making the
team, at least. You've got your nest egg no matter what."

"I wouldn't count on that. I'm sure that if I don't qualify he will find a way to take it away from me," Cole
replied.

"I suppose you might be right. In that case, I propose
a toast to the Cole Harrison Olympics," I declared supportively.

"And to our new home in Lakefront Village," Cole
added.

"Lakefront Village?" I asked after we drank.

"Yes, it's what I'm thinking of calling the development. What do you think?" Cole asked before adding,
"Before you answer, I want you to think about one more
question as well."

Cole reached into the inside pocket of his tuxedo.
With his other hand he reached across the table and took
one of mine. He placed a small jewelers box before me. I
was momentarily stunned. Part of me wanted to think it
was what I dreamed of, an engagement ring. But I
couldn't let myself get hurt by such false hope. I tried to
think of what else it might be. A necklace? Earrings?

Then I opened it. I couldn't believe my eyes! A giant
diamond engagement ring sparkled within. Cole looked

into my green eyes, smiled, and said: "Kate Kilpatrick, Will you marry me?"

His proposal stunned me. I was overwhelmed, confused. I broke into tears, smiled helplessly and got up from the table. I hurriedly left the dining room, followed closely by an equally stunned Cole, and exited to a small terrace overlooking Little Traverse Bay.

On one hand I was elated. It was the ring I had hoped for and I had rarely seen Cole this happy and enthusiastic. Plus Four's generosity, although unexpected and suspect in motive, meant that Cole would become a permanent resident of Harbor Springs. My dream of becoming Mrs. Cole Harrison of Harbor Springs, Michigan could come true. All I had hoped for was mine for the taking if I just said "yes."

However, the legality of the Tawkenin title troubled me. Naming it Lakefront Village didn't change that; in fact, it intensified my worry. Furthermore, even if the Anabe couldn't produce a legal claim, I felt that they had a clear moral claim to Tawkenin. I did not understand how Cole could knowingly develop someone else's land. I expected such behavior from Four, but I had hoped Cole would be different, especially after our night of stargazing in Mackinaw City. But still, despite my reservations, I wanted to be supportive; I mean it wasn't like Cole stole the land. It was a gift. I was totally confused.

Then my thoughts turned to Aupetchi and our meeting on Bliss Beach. I didn't know then how to help him, but I believed his racing would somehow preserve Tawkenin. Tonight's news made that belief seem ludicrous. Not only would the race be meaningless, but my boyfriend and possible fiancé could well be the one who took it from him. If there really was a rock and a hard place, I was smack dab in the middle. I struggled mentally; I knew there had to be a solution.

Cole intuitively gave me space. He stood a good ten feet from me, leaning on the terrace rail, his back to the water. I finally walked to him and took him in my arms.

"Oh Cole, I've waited so long for this day," I began.

"Does that mean yes?" he asked tentatively.

"Shhh, let me finish," I continued, gently placing two fingers on his lips. "I have dreamed of becoming your wife almost since our first date three years ago. You know that. I don't hide my emotions well. I have also always hoped that we would be able to stay up here. Harbor Springs will always be my home. I love it here, for many reasons, most of which I don't think you know or fully understand. My family is here, my home is here, and most of all, this is where my father rests eternally. This is where I feel closest to him. I value each of these things, but it is even more than that. I believe I share a spirit with this land and with the lake. I feel as though I have always been and always will be a part of this area. May tells me that my emotions articulate the true definition of their term Tawkenin. In fact that's why the Anabe call their homeland that, because it expresses how they feel."

"I still don't get it Kate. We own Townowkin, or whatever it is. You can be here forever with me," Cole rationalized.

"I know," I said, "and that's the problem. You can't own Tawkenin. It shouldn't be done. Owning Tawkenin is like owning Maymegwan's soul, Aupetchi's soul, my soul, your soul and all the souls that ever have and ever will be part of this land, this lake. You shouldn't own souls."

I could see the disappointment in his face. He had just asked me to marry him and here I was talking about souls.

"Don't get me wrong, Cole. I'm not saying no - I'm just not saying yes yet. I need to think all this through. So much has happened tonight," I explained.

"I know Kate, and I understand, I think," Cole lied. "Take all the time you need. Just tell me now that you love me as much as I love you."

"Oh I do! I love you more than I can explain," I said enthusiastically. "It will all work out, you'll see. Let's just give it some time. Now do you think we can go and finish dinner?" I knew it might be awkward to dine together now, but there was always the chance that the night might improve after our candidness. I wanted to give Cole that option.

Cole smiled. "I think we can do that." The magic returned to the evening as we reveled in our first true declaration of love for each other. Despite our confusion we were both certain of our love for one another. I felt that we both hoped and believed that things would work out. I was almost certain they would, if I could just find a solution to the Tawkenin mess. And I knew there was one; I could feel it swirling in my head. But like a vapor, I could not grasp it, yet. Still I was certain enough to keep the ring, albeit in its box.

I even tried it on after returning to my home in Bliss. I held my fingers out and let the light catch the diamond. It was beautiful. I sighed, took it off and placed it back in the jewelry box.

"It's all coming together Aupetchi", I murmured aloud. "The spirits are with us all and our destiny is in their hands."

AUPETCHI

My stay at Waugoshance was almost over. A pair of warriors had canoed to my camp two days ago and told me that they would return with Maymegwan before the moon disappeared. I had three days left. Grandmother Moon had gradually decreased her radiance each evening, transferring her power to me. I got stronger each day and as I did, her brilliance diminished. Last night she was a sliver in the night sky.

I now swam with the Grandmother Moon's spirit. This made me feel happy, strong and proud. I knew this would please Sawgemay. I was confident.

My swim today was in the warmest water yet: a thermometer would have recorded the water temperature at sixty-eight degrees. Still I covered my body with bear fat, as had become habit, before I swam. I entered the water and swam a half-mile through shallow open water to Kezhekekee. Still swimming, I followed the southern shore of the island and then crossed large windswept bay. I entered a shallower area that led me to Waugoshance.

As I began to circle the island, my mind wandered; slowly I recalled a strange experience that happened just two nights earlier.

After returning to camp that evening I quickly revived my banked embers into a small fire. I felt particularly swift in the water that day and I returned to camp with the sun higher in the sky than ever before. I let the warm sun dry me, as I positioned my soup kettle above the fire, stocked with a broth of roots, vegetables, grasses, and herbs. The kettle simmered perpetually during my stay. Periodically I would add remains of fish I netted or game I trapped, after trimming and roasting the meat.

That night I roasted duck. I crouched and watched the fat liquefy and drip into the fire. As each drop fell the fire intensified briefly, only to return to its steady yet chaotic burn. Each day here had been exhausting and this had been no exception. I looked forward to a good night's sleep wrapped in my thick deerskin robes. This was how I exorcised the chill of my daily swim from my body. It was an exorcism that was never quite complete; I was always cold.

My thoughts returned to the present as I rounded the island's southeastern point. The swells became bigger and I adjusted my rhythm. No longer needing to navigate the shoals and shallows, I could now do what I did best: ride the swells. I used a strong kick and deep pulls going up, then an easy kick with a short quick pull going down. Once I established this repetitive tempo my mind wandered back to the steady burn of my fire two nights ago.

I realized something then, while watching the flame and patiently letting the duck roast. It struck me slowly, like a shadow moving across the land as the sun appears from behind a cloud. It was actually a stretch that evoked the realization: As I stepped away from the fire to ease the stiffness from my crouched muscles, I became aware of a sensation long forgotten. I searched my memory and it came to me as I completed my stretch: warmth, I was warm. It had taken close to two weeks, but for the first time since I had arrived here, I was not cold. As that evening ended I did not need my thick layer of deerskin robes to keep me warm. Instead, I slept uncovered under the warm July night sky.

The next morning a second revelation came to me. After I recognized the warmth that enveloped me, I decided to take a run along the shoreline to celebrate, playfully skipping across a small brook that drained into Michi Gama. I let out a cheery whoop as I ran.

My joyous exclamation startled something in the grass to my side. I looked along the bank of the brook and saw a muskrat scurry away. I stopped in my tracks; muskrat stopped too. Our eyes met. Each held the gaze.

Then, after many moments passed, muskrat turned and continued on his way. I was certain he had smiled at me. I was certain muskrat had looked into my soul.

Even today as I re-approached Kezhekekee I felt muskrat with me, helping me to swim effortlessly. I increased my pace and quickly reached the shallow water close to shore. Usually I would wait until much later before exerting this energy; today I did it before I was three quarters of the way through my swim. Clearly I was getting stronger. I knew it, and most importantly, muskrat knew it. This was a very good sign because muskrat was a highly revered creature to my people, all because of his actions during a great flood.

Long ago Manitou became frustrated with his creations on Earth. He caused a great flood to cover the land, eradicating the bad. According to Anabe tradition, all men died and all the land creatures perished. Only the water creatures survived.

After the rains stopped a lonely old sprit woman lamented this tremendous loss of human life. This saddened Manitou, so he sent her a spirit man for companionship. They became close, coupled, and then he left. She bore twins: one a pure spirit and the other a physical being. Being of opposite natures they battled constantly and eventually killed each another. Once again, old woman was sad.

The water creatures had witnessed the explosive final battle in the sky. They saw the lonely, despondent spirit woman moping in the sky world afterwards. They tried to ease her pain. All of the water creatures gathered and persuaded a giant sea turtle to rise from the depths. They offered this turtle to her as a home in the middle world, between the sky world and the underneath world. Their generosity touched spirit woman, who needed a change, so she agreed to live on the giant turtle's back.

I finished my swim around Kezhekekee and crossed into open water again. I understood spirit woman's loneliness as she moved to her turtle home. It motivated me now. My solitary stay at Waugoshance had taught me how unnatural loneliness was, and how relentless you had to be to overcome it.

Tradition told us that she asked the water creatures to bring her some soil from the bottom of the great sea to build land on the turtle's back. One by one the animals tried. Beaver, marten, and loon each tried. Beaver, marten, and loon each failed.

"The water is too deep," they each said.

Finally, humble muskrat volunteered. Beaver, marten, and loon laughed at lowly muskrat.

"You are too weak," beaver said.

"You are foolish," loon crowed.

Muskrat ignored their taunts. He disappeared under the surface and the water creatures waited, for a long time. Muskrat did not reappear. Spirit woman's hope for soil upon which she could build a middle world faded. She was certain muskrat had perished in his foolhardy attempt.

Finally, after mourning had commenced, a ripple appeared on the surface. An object floated off in the distance. It did not move. Spirit woman went to explore, followed by the curious water creatures. It was muskrat, who was barely moving, but alive. Muskrat's clenched paw held a small bit of soil from the bottom of the sea. Mighty beaver, marten, and loon had failed. Only muskrat had succeeded.

The creatures revived muskrat, fed him, and reverently tended to him. Spirit woman took the small morsel of dirt and spread it on the great turtle's back. She breathed on it and the soil grew to form an island. Manitou sent spirit woman another companion. Soon all sorts of land creatures and human beings again populated the middle world, all because of the incredible endurance and indefatigable will of muskrat.

Now, as I approached my camp finishing my best swim yet, I understood what my earlier meeting with muskrat meant. When muskrat smiled at me and held my gaze he had passed to me his greatest gift: endurance. This pleased me. I felt doubly blessed as I prepared to return to Tawkenin. Not only did I feel warm again, but I had also discovered the endurance needed for my quest. Sawmay would deem my Waugoshance expedition a success.

Chapter Seven

WAXING QUARTER

Wednesday, August 2

AUPETCHI

My solitary training regimen ended simply. A single canoe arrived at my camp late in the evening. Among the travelers was my sister, Maymegwan. She was returning from another trade journey to Mackinaw City and her spirits were high, as were those of the crew who accompanied her.

"Aupetchi, you brought me good luck," May exclaimed as she raced to greet me.

"Your kind words touch me," I replied, "but it was not I who brought you your success in business."

"Oh but you did. I am filled with joy, so I know your time here has gone well," she explained. We believed that emotion was communal. Joy was shared, as was sorrow. May's success told her that my training had gone well.

The entourage that accompanied her gathered around my fire. I did not boast about my revelations nor did I openly display my improved physical prowess. The visitors quickly added fuel to the flame and quietly started a meal. We spent the evening in celebration, feasting on roast Mackinac venison and fresh Waugoshance lake trout. Murmurs rumbled among the group, noting my toned body and commenting on my peaceful resolve. I spent my last night at Waugoshance feeling physically fit and mentally satiated.

The expedition back to Tawkenin began at dawn. I was eager to return home and instructed the crew to paddle furiously throughout the hot, humid day so that we could beach by sunset. During the journey May and I huddled together in the center of the large canoe. No one asked either of us to paddle; our spirits had to remain pure. We fell into familiar and deep conservation.

"May, have you heard from your friend Kate?" I asked.

"Yes, I have," she nodded.

"Has she said anything about the race?" I continued.

"The big swim race? She did, actually. She told me about your meeting on Bliss Beach, when you both sought guidance from your ancestors," she replied. "Kate understands our way so well, don't you think?"

"She seems to be wise in that way, yes," I answered. "But in other ways I think she is not so smart. Like her choice of men."

"You know I agree, and I have some troubling news about her and Cole," May said. "He has asked her to marry him."

"Marry him?" I exclaimed. "But he is loud in voice, and weak in spirit."

"Well, she hasn't said yes yet. She wants him to prove his character to her first."

"Character? What is character?" I asked.

"We think of it as strength of spirit. The *waubesh* call it character," she explained. "But wait, there's more news, much worse news than that. She also said Cole now owns Tawkenin."

"What? That cannot be so," I frowned.

This news stunned me. I felt betrayed. It appeared that Kate was not only going to marry a bad man, but that she supported his stealing our land. Maymegwan quickly addressed the latter concern.

"But it's not all bad news. Kate told me she believes that if you win the race against Cole, we can keep Tawkenin."

"I don't see how that can be," I replied. Maymegwan explained it to me.

"Kate told me how she encouraged you to race, how she believed it would help save Tawkenin. Now she is sure of it."

"Sure of it?" I questioned. "How can she be?"

"Yes, now listen to me," she pleaded. "She explained that this could work perfectly for everyone. She can arrange things so that we can keep Tawkenin and she can have Cole prove his character to her. She is going to ask him to bet on the race."

"Bet on it?"

"Yes, brother. Cole loves to bet, she says. So she is go-ing to convince him that if you beat him, we will get their title to Tawkenin," May explained.

"So it is as she said on the beach, and as Saymay has foreseen," I reviewed aloud. "If I win this race I will pre-serve Tawkenin for the Anabe, for our people."

"Exactly,' said May.

"And if I lose?" I asked. "Or what if I win and he doesn't give me the title? Many *waubesh* lie to the Anabe."

"To the Anabe yes," May said, "to the woman they want to marry, no. If you win I am sure he will honor his word. He has to for Kate to marry him."

"I see," I mulled. "It is strange isn't it, the way of the *waubesh*? Why marry a man with weak spirit when you can choose whom to marry? Throughout the ages our an-cestors have chosen who goes with whom. A mate is paired with someone of equal spirit. Isn't ours a better way, to let the wisdom of the grandparents guide innocent youth? Only they are wise enough to see the strength of one's spirit."

"For our people, yes," May answered, "ours is truly a better way. I will follow the path chosen by my elders even though I walk often on the path of the *waubesh*. For the *waubesh*, however, I think ours is not the best way. For they see not only what you are; they also look at what you could become."

I pondered this for a few minutes. I knew that unlike most Anabe, Maymegwan understood the mind of the *waubesh* well.

"So your friend Kate is in love with what the loud boy will become?" I asked.

"Exactly," May replied.

"And if he agrees to race me for Tawkenin, this will help him to become who he will be," I concluded.

"That's it," she said.

I nodded. "I believe I understand. We all have different ways. Bear sleeps through the winter while deer forages amongst the snow."

"Exactly!"

"And I will be helping the loud boy to become who he can be, which will make your friend Kate happy."

"Very happy," May replied.

"May Manitou be with us," I concluded.

"Indeed," May agreed, then added, "and you, my brother better not lose."

COLE

Summer season was in full force. The White Pine restaurant sometimes had a seventy-minute wait. You would
think this would have annoyed me, but it did not. Curiously, Kate's free time became more abundant the busier
they got. The reason was simple: the lunch rush was so
intense that it prohibited Kate from working double
shifts. Helen knew better than to risk fatiguing her best
floor manager. Instead of working dinner as she did in
early summer, Kate simply passed the keys to Helen at
five o'clock.

Kate had still not responded to my marriage proposal,
and I did not push for an answer. Not that I understood
Kate's reluctance, I did not. I simply accepted her desire
to reflect. Plus, I was certain she would eventually say
yes. Furthermore, our relationship had gone extremely
well since that awkward moment when she first failed to
reply. I didn't want to rock the boat. Besides, Kate chose
to spend her increased time off with me, so I figured the
future could wait. The present was pretty damn good.

A high point occurred during mid-July. I had joined
my parents at a dinner party they held for guests from
New York. They were genuine New York Knickerbockers,
meaning they were descendents of the first Dutch settlers
in the Hudson River valley. Jacob and Edith Van Schaick,
had come up north for a week. During this dinner they
paid Kate a great compliment.

"I must say that lunch at the White Pine was superb,
even better than dinner. We had such a delightful experience there today," Jacob had said to the group.

"Yes Elizabeth. You really must try it," Edith had
cooed in agreement, before turning to me. "I've heard that
you show the beautiful young lady who runs the White
Pine lunch around town from time to time."

"That I do. And she's a great friend, not like a local at
all," I had responded, somewhat defensively. "Tell me,
why was it so wonderful?"

"You mean you haven't eaten at the Inn?" Edith had said, feigning shock.

"Well no, I haven't. Kate says I would distract her."

"Well that just proves it," Jacob had lectured. "That kind of focus is why she runs the most efficient dining room on Little Traverse Bay. Good show."

This praise pleased me. I was proud and happy for Kate. I was proud to be "showing her around," as Edith so quaintly phrased it.

◆◆◆

Four and Elizabeth had invited Kate to the Harrison "cottage" twice since my *soiree* with the Van Schaicks. I was certain that the praise they had for her prompted these invitations. Both times it was to small dinner parties of ten people. Kate found my parents to be polite and entertaining hosts, which surprised me. During the second dinner my parents took particular pleasure in Kate's ability to converse with a bus boy in his native tongue.

Bradford needed help for these dinner parties so my parents hired a local to bus tables, do dishes, and help where needed. His name was named Penay, and he was Native American. It didn't occur to me that he was an Anabe until this particular evening. Sometimes I just didn't catch on.

Anyway, during the meal Penay came in to clear the main course. We had enjoyed roast prime rib from Texas, fresh minced horseradish from a farm market in Traverse City, mashed Idaho potatoes, and fresh Michigan green beans. Moving stiffly in his white linen uniform, he approached Kate and asked if she was finished.

"*Newesin peto wishkobun meno auwaysin, nekawnes,*" answered Kate, looking Penay squarely in the eye.

An obviously startled Penay briefly returned her stare.

"*Newob kagete, omesayemaw,*" Penay replied, slightly ruffled and completely captivated by Kate's warm, welcoming gaze.

After a brief pause the Anabe composed himself. He

moved to clear Four's plate. "Will there be anything else sir?" he asked.

"Yes, tell Bradford that we will have dessert and coffee on the patio in fifteen minutes."

"Yes sir," Penay replied and returned to the kitchen.

"That was quite impressive Miss Kilpatrick," my mother said when he was gone. "How is that you speak the Chippewa tongue? Please share the nature of your conversation."

"Of course Mrs. Harrison. Actually, Penay is Anabe. The Chippewa lived further south, along the Lake Huron shore," Kate explained. "Northern Michigan, the Upper Peninsula, and much of the northern Lower Peninsula was Ojibwa land, and the Anabe belong to the Ojibwa nation."

"How interesting," Elizabeth replied. "I never realized they were such a complicated people. Now do tell us what you said."

"Of course, and please forgive my unsolicited lecture. It was presumptuous of me."

"Not at all Miss Kilpatrick. Please continue," Four interjected, impressed by her acquiescence.

"Certainly and thank you. I expressed to Penay that I was eating a delicious and well-prepared meal," Kate explained.

"Well done Miss Kilpatrick. When in Rome I suppose," Four replied.

"Indeed," added Elizabeth. "I often hear them in the kitchen speaking to each other, and I recognize the phrase you said to Penay. It sounded like nee-kawn-ess. What does that mean?"

"You have a very good ear Mrs. Harrison," complemented Kate. "I addressed him as brother, *nekawnes.* He responded by calling me sister, *omesayemaw.* It's a courtesy that I find most welcome."

"That is nice. Of course, you are not related to him are you?" Elizabeth asked, a little less than discreetly.

"In friendship only. My good friend Maymegwan is

Penay's cousin. Since May and I are close, the Anabe consider me one of their own. Penay knows me through her."

◆◆◆

This exchange encouraged me, as did her equally successful first dinner. Despite this performance, Four and
Elizabeth remained neutral about Kate. Her social and
language skills exceeded their expectations, but her familiarity with the "Indians" kept many of their
reservations intact. She was, once they boiled it all down,
still just a local girl.

Not that I cared what they thought about her; I loved
Kate and if all went well they would have to accept her as
one of their own. At the very least I knew that her natural
grace and her ability to engage in conversation effortlessly made her a welcome, albeit not beloved, guest at
the Harrison dinner table. That would suffice for now; one
step at a time.

Meanwhile, Olivia had increased me to two-a-day
workouts. I swam every morning from nine to eleven;
mostly distance with moderate rest and some kicks and
pulls. Then Olivia and I ate together at noon, with
Winston and Elizabeth if they were home, before returning to the pool at two-thirty. It was hot then, but it was
really Olivia who made the sacrifice; I was in the pool after all. And if it were too hot she would join me.

I was usually done by four-thirty, after which I would
shower, shave, and drive my Roadster, obediently, to the
White Pine's employee's entrance.

On this night we were headed to an activity common
to the many beaches of Michigan whenever the nights
were cool, the sky was clear, the water fresh and the beaches
broad. If you flew at a low altitude above the sandy Lake Michigan
shoreline on any clear summer night, an illuminating path
of bonfires would guide you. Every four or five miles you
would come across a raging pile of dried pine, cedar, cherry and
birch casting irregular light on an ever-changing crowd of
people.

The crowds could include anyone between the ages of one to one hundred, sitting in the sand or upon a variety of makeshift driftwood benches. The fifteen to fifty-year-olds who represented the majority drank beer or wine, sang, fought, flirted, and made love, sometimes in that order. It didn't matter who you were or where you came from; bonfire parties had few social barriers. Everyone was welcome. All were anonymous.

We had eaten at the Park House Hotel in neighboring Petoskey. I had a steak while Kate nibbled at perch. Then we drove to Five-Mile Point just outside Harbor Springs, where a beach fire blazed under the bright light of the waxing moon. The sun had set just before ten o'clock. Young teens had arrived at the fire before us, sneaking out from under the watchful eyes of their parents. They had started the fire, then guzzled a few six-packs of beer. Most had stumbled home within a few hours. A gang of unemployed locals arrived next, aimlessly combing the beaches for activity and action. The lure of the fire enabled them to mingle easily. Near midnight hospitality staff from the closing restaurants and bars started to arrive. The pace picked up noticeably. Most were downstaters working up north for the summer. A fair mix of locals arrived with them, mostly customers from the closing taverns looking for the party to continue. This was when we arrived.

This fire was far from the beach access road. The isolated location created a mysterious atmosphere that Kate and I appreciated. As we approached the fire, the shadowy light of the flames revealed brief glimpses of the dynamic crowd. Smell followed sight and the refreshing scent of blazing kindling reached us. Our ears prickled at the crackle and hiss of burning wood. Above us, an umbrella of starlight never seen in any city covered us, unmolested by the descending crescent moon.

KATE

I left work feeling blue, having concluded that my position as Dining Room Supervisor was no longer challenging. Rewarding, yes - challenging, no. I had developed strong interpersonal communication skills, had a solid understanding of accounting fundamentals, and possessed the ability to organize and plan for each and every day. I was good at my job, and it had become nearly easy. My mother said I had flexible consistency. I thought of it as common sense.

I started each season by training my lunch staff for two full days. First I oriented them to the work place. I reviewed the menu, taught them how to place an order and demonstrated proper service procedures. I outlined the White Pine's service and food quality standards and reviewed the staff handbook. I gave them a thorough tour of the operation. Throughout the program I engaged them in various team building and motivational exercises. Most of my mom's dinner crew, despite being long-time employees, joined us.

"It doesn't matter if you're talking to a customer, conversing with a peer, directing a subordinate, listening to a supervisor, or patiently giving a fudgie directions to a competitor. Every effort should be made to ensure that their experience is a positive one," I preached. "We should satisfy or surpass their expectations each and every time."

In addition, I kept meticulous records. I kept a log of our daily food and labor costs, tracked our sales religiously and insisted on a weekly inventory of meat, produce and liquor. I recorded the weather, noted significant local events and calculated the individual productivity of each server.

I revised the dining room schedule weekly, using my most recent calculations to forecast my staffing needs. I tried to always have the exact number of servers needed on the floor, never too few or too many. This investment

in planning and analysis made my success appear effortless. I did the job so well that the dining room seemed to
run itself. Consequently, the challenge was gone.

So my dinner with Cole at the Park House had been
extremely welcome, and pleasant. The day's events easily
drifted from my mind and I was not thinking of work at
all when we approached the beach bonfire. I focused upon
the firelight reflecting off the calm lake water.

We walked slowly, aimlessly. The firelight grew more
intense as we moved closer. Halfway there we detoured
into the pine forest that bordered the sandy beach and
found a small, secluded vale between the dunes. The lake
breeze whistled through the branches high above us. The
beach grass surrounding us flowed like waves upon a
lake. We held each other close, kissed each other tenderly
and silently watched the crescent moon seemingly melt
into the lake. An hour later we returned to the beach
where both the fire and the party were raging.

When we reached the pyre I drifted over to a group of
locals clustered upwind, away from the smoke. I had
known these people since birth. They look downwind with
amusement at the so-called smoked fudgies. This was a
long-standing joke among us locals, who marveled at the
tendency of the tourists to congregate downwind, in the
thick haze. Tonight was no different; the positioning
around the fire was well established and time honored.

Cole appreciated the status afforded those who stood
upwind. Truth be known, I suspect it was one of the reasons he first approached me. He knew that by dating a
local he could stand with the locals. His cleverness impressed me. There was no other way to get out of the
smoke; even the Harrison fortune couldn't break this class
barrier. His strategy worked, and my smoke-free clique
welcomed us both warmly. However, our visit was brief
since I avoided mingling too long with my staff, which was
present in full force.

Which isn't to say I didn't like them, for I did, dearly. The problem was that unlike most seasonal managers I knew it was easier to supervise acquaintances than friends. So I acknowledged them casually, then led Cole through the crowd. We stopped to talk to another couple, which was a rarity at a beach fire. Most partygoers were single - at least they were when they arrived. A local named Richie Wilson greeted us.

Richie was with one of Cole's neighbors from the point, Eleanor MacKenzie. Eleanor's grandfather had founded Canada's MacKenzie Oil Company. The four of us stood alone, between the locals and the fudgies. Eleanor looked uncomfortable, and with good reason. The locals did not accept her like they did Cole. Not only did her wealth make her stand out but her arrogance also distanced her from Richie's friends. One of Cole's good qualities was that he was not arrogant about his wealth; instead, he was embarrassed by it. Despite living on adjacent properties, Eleanor and Cole knew each other only socially at best.

On the other hand, Richie and I knew each other quite well. We met in the first grade and had moved through the Harbor Springs school system together. His father ran a successful service station in downtown Harbor Springs and Richie was his top mechanic. Cole knew him too, as he kept Cole's Buick running smooth.

"Rich-ie, the man who keeps my Roadster running!" Cole exclaimed as he warmly shook Richie's hand.

"Cole Harrison," Richie responded while passing a cold Stroh's long neck to Cole and I from his ever-present cooler, "good to see you man. I hear you've been driving her up to Mackinaw City. She must be due for a tune-up."

"You're probably right Rich, although she's running great," Cole agreed.

"Well he won't be going to Mackinaw City much anymore," I interjected. "Mom's finally giving me some nights off and I intend to keep him close to home."

"That sounds wonderful," Eleanor said. "Just don't distract him from the swimming pool. Cole is defending the Point's honor on Labor Day and he must not lose to a local. It wouldn't be right."

I bristled at Eleanor's demeaning comment and looked at Richie from the corner of my eye. As expected, he hadn't caught her slam.

"That's right man. You're going to kick some ass!" Richie confirmed loudly.

Local opinion was unanimous when it came to Eleanor MacKenzie. Townspeople felt she was using Richie, plain and simple. He was young, strong, handsome, and naive. He believed Eleanor when she told him she would leave her social position and affluent lifestyle to live with him forever as a gas station owner's wife. The townspeople did not. Locals understood that Richie was not the sharpest tack on the board.

Eleanor could be very convincing, but I knew she would never leave high society. I sometimes worked the *soirees*, dances and dinners that filled Harbor Point's social calendar each season so I often saw Eleanor in her full glory. She would invariably arrive on the arm of what the locals called "fresh bait," a new young man futilely trying to meet her impossible marital qualifications. Each was rich, most were reasonably well-behaved, and a few were genealogically appropriate. None made it past her initial cut. No man had escorted her twice, and never did she arrive with Richie. He was her after-party toy.

I once told Cole I was going to tell Richie the truth. Cole convinced me otherwise. It would be pointless, he explained, because Eleanor would just find another local boy to "slum" with. I would be transferring, not solving the problem. Plus, Eleanor's generosity exceeded her insincerity so Richie was getting a taste of the good life, probably for the only time in his life. Cole also felt that Richie's even-temper would serve him well when she did inevitably leave him.

He also thought Richie's friends would stand by him,
so Eleanor wouldn't shatter his psyche permanently. He
might be temporarily confused at worst. And she would
give him money when she was done with him, less than a
fortune but more than a pittance. Cole reasoned that
Richie would survive better than most. Cole also knew
that regardless of how Eleanor treated him, a number of
local women would eagerly ease his pain when she was
done. Even tonight they postured around him, letting
him know that when he was ready, they were willing and
able.

I bit my lip thoughtfully as I reflected upon the couple. I disagreed with Cole completely. I felt Richie should
know and resented Cole for persuading me not to tell him.
It had been one of our tough moments together, and now
that memory filled my mind. My thoughts were far from
the fire and our immediate company.

Why were Cole and I so different? And since we were
so different should I accept his proposal? Wouldn't he
grow tired of me and eventually dispose of me? Worse
yet, would he eventually love me only as the mother of our
children, not as the object of his passion? I knew that
Four and Elizabeth would always dictate that even if he
was unhappy he must keep me as his wife forever for appearance's sake, and to help raise "his" children. I did not
want to be trapped in an unhappy marriage.

I saw outwardly jovial, inwardly miserable young
couples like that every day at the White Pine Inn. Most
came from the Point. I had no desire to be a part of it.
Seeking solace, or reassurance, I turned and looked into
Cole's eyes, trying to see into his soul and uncover answers to my questions. Instead, Cole squinted past me,
peering through the smoke into the haze-covered crowd.

"Jay? Jay! Jay Pond, it is you, you son of a bitch."

Cole bolted past the bonfire and into the swarm of
smoked fudgies. He grasped the right hand of a tall, red-
faced, blond-haired young man who slapped Cole on the
back.

"Cole Harrison, I thought I might run into you up here," the man exclaimed.

"Damn right," Cole replied. "So how are you Jay?"

"Good Cole, thanks," Jay smiled.

"So what are you up to? Are you still playing life-guard?" Cole asked with more than a little disdain.

"That I am," Jay acknowledged, "but not today and tomorrow. I'm visiting some friends on Paradise Lake."

"Excellent. It's good to see you," Cole replied. "Now come out of the smoke and meet the gang."

Jay was much more than a lifeguard. Not yet nine-teen, he was the youngest member of a vanishing breed. For more than a century, lifesaving stations operated by the U.S. Lifesaving Corps had dotted the Great Lakes' coastline. This prestigious group kept watch over the inland seas' most treacherous passages. Their purpose was simple: to assist the many ships that floundered an-nually along the coast.

Steel hull ships with improved communications were rendering the Corps obsolete. Radio technology warned mariners of upcoming squalls before their arrival. Only a few wooden schooners remained, and most of them were sleek clippers. Powerboats using a variety of fuel sources dominated the lakes. This plethora of small crafts easily found safe harbor before weather troubles exploded. The steel giants altered their paths, at best, and only in the most violent winter storms. Usually they just plodded purposefully through the tempests. The corps was no longer needed.

Jay worked at the life saving station located at Sleep-ing Bear Bay, which was scheduled to be one of the last to close. Wooden coal barges still steamed up to the D.H. Day dock to unload fuel for the giant lakers. Occasionally they faltered, so the Corps still saw action there, albeit limited.

Jedediah Pond was Jay's father and the station com-

mander. He had employed his only son for the past four
years. This would be their last together. The two men
were similar in stature: Jay stood at over six feet tall and
weighed close to 200 pounds, all of it muscle. Despite their
similarities and his father's high reputation though, Jay
had earned his place on the Corps with his ability, not his
genealogy. He was easily the most enthusiastic and ar-
guably the most capable member of the Corps.

Jay would have followed in his father's career path
had circumstance permitted, for like Jedediah, the ro-
mance of the lake seduced him completely. In fact he
distinctly recalled the moment the lakes claimed his soul:
It was when his father took him scuba diving for the first
time, when he was ten years old.

They had prepared for the event for a month.
Jedediah devoted ten hours a week to Jay's training. By
the time they were finished Jay could scuba like others
snorkeled, snorkel like others swam, and swim like others
walked. He had a "feel" for the water. Father and son
hitched their eight-foot rowboat to their government-issue
jeep and towed it across the narrow northern tip of Michigan's Lower Peninsula. They drove to Rogers City, on the
shores of Lake Huron, where they launched the craft.

A ten horsepower outboard puttered them bravely
into the waters of Duncan Bay. Jedediah selected this bay
because of the numerous shipwrecks that littered its shallow waters. They were mostly small wooden scows with a
few large barges mingled in, most of which were used to
haul the limestone that was quarried nearby. Jedediah
knew the location of twenty-one ships. The wreck they
were to visit was more than 30 feet down and would be
invisible from their bobbing vessel.

Jedediah gave Jay last minute instructions as they
approached the dive site. The young boy was to stay close
to his father. They agreed upon hand signals that they
would use to communicate when submerged. It was late-
July so the water was warm; no wet suits were needed.
Long cotton swimsuits would suffice just fine.

Jedediah entered the water first, stepping backwards off the craft. Jay followed him in, cleared his mask, and located his father in the haze of his new environment. Jedediah acknowledged his son with a hearty thumbs-up and the two began their descent. Their weight belts did the bulk of the work as they sank slowly to the bottom, yards from the wreck. Visibility was about 15 feet. Jay's heart raced. His father had not prepared him for this.

The water that enveloped them was surprisingly empty and terribly silent. All that surrounded them was cold, quiet liquid. Jay expected to see lots of fish swimming around him but there were none. It was all very disconcerting.

It had taken less than ninety seconds to descend and settle on the sandy bottom. To Jay it had felt like hours. Jedediah checked the air tanks and signaled for Jay to clear and reseal his mouthpiece. Once accomplished, they swam easily towards the wreck. Their arms dangled along their sides as they let their flippers propel them. The swimming calmed Jay, as it was the only sensation familiar to him in this foreign environment.

The mask restricted his peripheral vision and the lake water was murky, at best. He could not hear a thing. The realization that sound could not travel in the deep overwhelmed him. It was more than quiet. The environment was vacuous. The water enclosed him. His every move met with resistance and required specific, thoughtful effort. The environment even altered Jay's sense of taste. The hard rubber mouthpiece reminded him of the rubber erasers he used to chew on in school. It was truly another world.

Jay looked about him and the desolation seemed absolute. There was nothing to see. No seaweed - in fact, no plants at all - no rocks, no pebbles, no crustaceans, no fish, no coral, no nothing. Just sand and water and quiet. He settled into a rhythm as he followed his father through the pressurized liquid atmosphere. Jay's vision focused upon his father's feet as they moved easily forward below the surface. In a few minutes his father stopped and signaled to Jay; they were getting close to the wreck. Jay could see nothing. He shrugged his shoulders with resignation and turned to his left. Then, without warning, something knocked his facemask ajar. He cleared it quickly, only to find himself face-to-face with a twenty-five pound lake trout.

Suddenly, unexpectedly, life appeared beneath the waves. Jay looked beyond the trout and saw hundreds of fresh water fish busily feeding. Now he knew where the life was and saw that it was plentiful, albeit congested. Pike, perch, bass, and trout of all sizes and ages dominated the scene. Jedediah caught Jay's eye and led him into the heart of activity. Jay quickly saw what the cause of the gathering was: the ghostly remains of the *Northern Spirit*.

The wood barge had floundered sixty years earlier. The keel was intact but the beam had collapsed chaotically. The wreckage created a protective, shadowed reef that served as an oasis on the desolate lake bottom. A small bit of the fo'c'sle remained which the pair excitedly explored. It was magnificent. For the first time in his life Jay fully understood what thrilling, wonderful, and awesome meant. The dive lasted about twenty minutes and changed Jay's life. He would view the world with different eyes from that day on. It was as though the soul of a lost crewmember lived within him. This experience connected him eternally to the lake and then, logically, to his father's vocation.

When I learned this about Jay it impressed me greatly, as it revealed much about his character. To Cole however, this was not impressive at all. To him Jay Pond was a decent swimmer who watched for shipwrecks that no longer occurred.

◆◆◆

Cole led Jay through the milling crowd and rejoined

us. He introduced him to Richie, Eleanor and me. Then Cole explained that Jay had been his swim rival for over ten years.

"In fact, Jay's sister Emma was Olivia's nemesis for years," Cole explained.

"That's right," Jay teased, "and I've beaten Cole almost as much as Emma beat Olivia."

"As if, Pond, you scum!" Cole exclaimed. "Olivia owned Emma and you know it."

"Well, maybe in college but Emma was unbeatable when she was young."

"True enough," Cole agreed. "How is she these days?"

"Great. She's married and living in Grand Haven, with my first nephew on the way."

"Cool. I'll tell Olivia. I just hope the poor kid doesn't end up as another shipwreck lifeguard," Cole replied. "Three loser's per family is too many."

I bristled at his tactless remark and tried to smooth the situation. I also sensed that my opportunity had arrived.

"So Jay, will we see you in two weeks at the Water Wonderland swimming meet?" I asked.

"You will," he answered.

"Oh good. What will you be swimming?" I continued.

"The same stuff: the 50, 100 and a couple of relays. After all, I've got to extend my win streak against Harrison here. What is it now Cole, five in a row?"

"More like three. Too bad though, I'll be swimming the 200 and 400."

"Oh, I see, ducking me, eh Harrison?" Jay jeered.

"You wish," Cole said defensively.

"Actually," Eleanor interrupted, "if you must know, Jay, Cole is training to win an open water race up here during our Labor Day festival. Isn't that right Cole?"

"Distance? An open water swim?" Jay taunted. "That's got to be at least two or three miles, Cole doesn't even do a mile in his workouts. He's a sprinter like me."

"Don't worry Pond, I plan on beating your butt in the sprints for years to come," Cole answered, "but I'm also shooting for the Olympics. So I'm going to race some distance. Olivia is working with me on my endurance. Then I can make Pond scum at any distance."

"Okay smartass," Jay bristled at the continued slurs, "if you won't swim me in the Water Wonderland, I'll come up here and smoke you in the open water. When is it? Labor Day weekend?"

"That's right," Cole spouted, "and what say we make it interesting and put a little wager on it this time."

"Sure thing Harrison," Jay agreed. "I've got $20 that says I'll beat you."

"$20, is that all? I'll see your $20 and raise you $200," Cole countered.

"No way. I don't have that kind of jack," Jay replied.

"Oh that's all right. When I win I'll just take your $20. If you win, and that isn't going to happen, I'll give you $200," Cole said. "Fair enough, Pond?"

"Fair enough," he agreed.

"Great. Let's close the deal with a few beers."

"Sure enough," Jay said, "sure enough."

Now I knew my opportunity had arrived. I sensed that my father's spirit and the sprits of Aupetchi's ancestors were with me.

Five beers later Cole's rivalry with Jay was a distant memory. The barley and hops made him sentimental. We linked arms and followed Eleanor and Richie into the night and back to our waiting cars. The good-byes that followed were warm. Soon I was cautiously navigating the Roadster home as Cole dozed happily beside me. After a while he awoke, and I turned to him.

"Cole, why did you to bet on the race?" I inquired.

"It makes it more interesting, babe. Plus I know I'll smoke Pond," he boasted.

"I don't doubt it hon. You're swimming so well. I was

wondering if you'd be interested in another wager? On the race, that is."

"I might. The only place I can get away with it is up here. But who else would be stupid enough to bet me? I'm the fastest man up north," he responded confidently.

"Probably, but do you remember May's brother, Aupetchi?" I asked.

"The carver dude? Sure I do," Cole said sarcastically. "He wants to bet? What's he going to wager, one of his trinkets?"

"Actually no. And don't be fooled Cole, Aupetchi is smart and he can swim. He wants to race you for the deed to the land your father wants you to develop, Tawkenin."

"No shit, really?" Cole asked. "I don't get it."

"Sweetie, people live on that land, lots of people, people I care about. You can't just force them to move. They will fight you every step of the way, in court and even man-to-man if they have to. It won't be easy, no matter what your father says. They won't just leave," I explained.

"But we have legal title," Cole said.

"Not according to them," I replied. "Plus, if they fight you, it will take you many years, tons of money, and lots of bad publicity to get clear title. The locals are loyal to the Anabe; your reputation and your family name will suffer."

"So what? We can afford it and I have plenty of years to fight it. We'll sell to down-staters that don't know an Anabe from an Ohioan. The money we'll make is worth the wait," he reasoned.

"True enough Cole. I can't argue with that," I said. "The thing is, if you do go through with this and fight to take that land away, I can never marry you. I am one of those people who understand the good the Anabe do for us here."

"What? Are you saying that if I develop this land you won't marry me? That's why you're hesitant?"

"Not exactly honey," I sighed, "I'm saying that if you

fight to develop it - that is, if you take it from them - you will prove to me that you are not the man I want to marry. My husband must posses a sense of honor; he must understand that taking land against the will of the people who live upon it is immoral. Your father would fight to develop the land; that's who he is. I just hope and pray that it is not who you are."

"Well, I don't want to be like Four, that's for sure," Cole mused thoughtfully. "So you're saying that if I beat Aupetchi he will give me my land honorably? He can guarantee me that his people will not fight the development, that they will leave peacefully and willingly?"

"That's right. He has the blessing of his people, provided you agree to give up your claim to the land if he wins. It is an honorable solution to a dishonorable situation."

"Hmm," Cole murmured, "that does seem honorable. And when I win you will accept my proposal?"

"I will, for that will show me that Cole Harrison is not Four Harrison, that you will not become your father."

Cole reflected for a moment, turned to me and smiled enthusiastically.

"All right then, I'll do it."

Chapter Eight

WANING QUARTER

Wednesday, August 16

AUPETCHI

I was swimming six miles a day since my return from Waugoshance, three starting at dawn and three ending at dusk. Michi Gama had been unusually calm, her water exceptionally warm. Manitou clearly swam with me. The Anabe who watched me train knew it to be true.

Still Sawmay was concerned. Only the wise man and I knew what was at stake. If I lost to Cole, Tawkenin would be lost forever, on Sawmay's watch. This would bring his family terrible shame and destroy the lives of our people. So Sawmay met with me my first two nights back, to evaluate my condition. He was pleased with my mental state. Despite this he continually monitored my physical readiness.

Sawmay woke each dawn, walked to the shoreline and discreetly watched me swim. I knew he was there, and the fact that he was comforted me. He had to be pleased with what he saw. I had never felt better. My movements were effortless and natural; I was one with the water.

This morning, like every morning, I had returned to my hut after my dawn swim and broken my nightlong fast with dried berries and smoked fish. Then I supplicated myself in a sweat lodge, praying for Manitou's continued approval. After my twilight swim I decided to return to the beach where Kate and I had met.

I took the animal trace that connected my village to Bliss Beach and eventually settled on a secluded dune to meditate. The dune was close to the house where Kate lived, hidden yet imminent. The sky was dark and the stars were bright. I sat for a moment before a beam of light broke the darkness. Someone was walking the beach, scanning the shore with a flashlight.

I remained silent as the body slowly moved towards me. The strolling figure's head was down but her curves revealed her gender and consequently her identity: it was Kate. She stopped periodically to look out on the lake, which was eerily still under the dark sky. Gentle, almost imperceptible undulation whispered from the shore. The Milky Way glowed directly above us, overwhelming the falcate moon.

Finally she stopped and crouched directly in front of my hidden shelter. She delicately picked up a small stone and held it to the light. She turned it slowly, and then dipped it into the water.

"Greeting sister," I whispered. "May I see your stone?"

Kate turned to the dunes. Her demeanor was calm, not startled or scared. She recognized my voice. I climbed down from the shelter of the dune and joined her on the shore. She handed me the stone. It was a Petoskey stone. I dipped it into the water and then held it out for her to illuminate with the light.

"This is very good," I said while nodding towards the small treasure.

"It is beautiful isn't it?" Kate asked.

"Yes," I agreed, "it is flawless."

"I would like you to have it," she said, "so you can reveal the spirit within."

"Thank you," I replied gratefully. "I will try."

I held the Petoskey stone tightly in my hand and closed my eyes. I emptied my mind, permitting only the spirit of the stone to enter. Minutes passed before I spoke again.

"It has your spirit, sister. I sense the grace of the heron and the beauty of a mink. Which would you prefer me to reveal?"

"Wow, now that's a tough choice."

I led her back to my dune where we sat together. We were both barefoot and we instinctively dug our toes into the sand. When we finished we looked at each other, looked down at our buried feet, glanced at one another again, and laughed. We were comfortable with each other, kindred spirits in a sacred place.

Time passed as we admired the sight of a distant freighter gliding silently under the hanging moon. Without speaking I placed my hand on Kate's. Without looking at me Kate smiled. Eventually she spoke again.

"So it's the heron or the mink? Graceful or cute? I don't know which is better," Kate pondered aloud.

"They each have many gifts," I noted.

"That they do," she agreed, "but I've always loved herons. They're so tolerant of others it seems."

She leaned back and drew her knees to her chest with her long tan arms. Sensing she would stay for a while, I stretched out and reclined on my side, facing her.

"I remember a family canoe trip when I was around five years old. I was sitting in the middle of a canoe while my parents paddled. My father was in the stern; he was always in the stern. My brothers were in their own canoes and had raced ahead of us. They were nowhere to be seen, which was good because my parents liked to move slowly. We drifted as much as possible."

"You see life on the river best when you move slowly," I mumbled.

Kate did not seem to hear me.

"We were cruising along and had just come around a long, lazy bend when we came upon a giant blue heron," she continued. "My father motioned for me to be still. He whispered that this was a father heron and that his nest was nearby. His mate was with their hatchlings. We drifted with the current and remained still. As we passed him he followed us closely, yet casually, out of the corner of his eye. He never looked directly at us. When we drifted by him he just stood there. I was sure he would try to scare us away, or else take flight. But he just stood there, calm and secure. I remember being very impressed and thinking that if I were baby heron I would want him to be my father."

"Yes, they are good parents," I said.

"Then, as we moved away I looked back and for the first time he looked right at us, catching my eye. We held each other's gaze briefly, and then he took wing and flew right over the canoe. My father, who had witnessed our exchange, dipped his head knowingly, winked, and smiled. He told me that the heron had picked me, and only me, as someone special, someone he could trust. He would now serve as my guardian."

"Much like Sawmay guides me," I reflected.

"A while later, farther downriver we came upon him again, and the same thing happened. He let us pass, took wing and flew downriver ahead of us. This dance contin-ued three or four times before he finally left us to our journey. Each time, our eyes met before he took wing. I feel that he has been with me ever since, watching over me, protecting me."

I gazed out over the water. I said nothing, yet knew that Kate knew I understood. I reopened my hand to re-veal the stone she had collected. I turned it over twice with my fingertips before nodding my head. Finally I faced her.

"The heron it is then," I declared.

"Thank you, you are very generous," Kate replied. "Now I have some news to share with you."

"Is it good news?" I asked.

"Yes Aupetchi, it is very good news. You will be pleased, as pleased as I am that you see my spirit in this stone."

KATE

I watched as Aupetchi carefully placed the Petoskey stone into a deerskin satchel, then I spoke once again. I was anxious to tell him the news.

"Cole accepted the wager," I said.

Aupetchi did not visibly react. He sat in silence. Finally he turned to me and looked directly into my eyes. I returned his gaze only to discover a smile emerging on his normally stoic face. I could no longer contain my happiness.

"Did you hear me Aupetchi? Tawkenin can remain forever Anabe!"

"Yes, this is so, but only if I can swim faster than your friend, and only if my will is strong," Aupetchi replied. "I am certain that I will be swift, for Manitou has joined my quest. I am less certain of my will. This wager makes me uneasy."

"But why, Aupetchi? This is what you wanted."

"That it is sister, that it is."

"Then why are you still troubled?"

Aupetchi did not immediately respond. He inhaled deeply, exhaled slowly. He gazed at the stars above him. I looked up as well. I noticed the twin stars in the handle of the Big Dipper, but only when I did not look directly at them. Eventually Aupetchi broke the silence.

"I understand you might marry this Cole Harrison, and I know you to be a woman of great spirit, Kate. So tell me this if you can. Do you believe this man-boy will do as he says, that he will give me claim to the land when I beat him?" Aupetchi asked. "For I worry that he will not. I do not see the character in him that you must. I see someone with a weak spirit."

I responded immediately.

"Aupetchi. Do you see that constellation above us? The one the we *waubesh* call the Big Dipper?" I asked.

"Yes, I see it, although our people see a bear, not a dipper," he answered.

"Really? You see a bear?"

"I do. I see him stalking his prey, night after night."

"Hmmm, I can see that a little myself. Do you see that bright star on its rear haunches?"

"I do," he said as he pointed above him.

"That's the one," I confirmed. "Now I want you to look at it while not really looking at it. Look to the southeast, and then try to see it out of the corner of your eye. We call that using your peripheral vision."

Aupetchi did as I asked, no doubt thinking that it was strange for the *waubesh* to have a name for this kind of looking. May had explained to me once how the Anabe tried to look everywhere at once, that they moved their eyes constantly through their field of vision. I could see he struggled to focus upon only one object. Then suddenly his head jerked. I watched as his eyes moved again and smiled when his head twitched anew.

"I see what I have not seen before. There are two stars where there appears to be one," Aupetchi marveled.

"Exactly." I confirmed. "We call them twin stars. There are two, but most people don't see them. It's a lot like the way you see Cole. Many people, you among them I fear, see only his wealth or his confidence and call it arrogance or brashness. They do not try to see him when they are not looking at him. I do. I have spent hours watching him when he does not know I am looking and I see what others cannot. Like the stars above us Cole, has another spirit: well hidden but as equally bright."

"I hope this is so," came the reply.

"The only problem is, I think it will remain hidden until a challenge forces him to reveal it to others," I explained. "It is my hope that this race will be that challenge."

"Perhaps. Like the star I have never seen before, this may be true," Aupetchi reassured me. "However I know that it is difficult to change spirit. This is true for people as well as places. Look at the village where you work, your Harbor Springs."

"What do you mean?" I asked quizzically.

"When my people first came to Tawkenin it was not our native land. We did not live here permanently. We came from another place, as you know."

"Yes I do, May has told me that."

"Did she tell you that before we lived here we used the land much as the *waubesh* use it now? We didn't live here, yet we hunted the forest and fished the water. We lived on the southern shore of Michi Gama, where She-gogong now stands."

"Yes. She told me that also."

"We wintered in Shegogong. In late spring we canoed to Tawkenin to plant and tend to our crops. We spent the summer up here, just as the *waubesh* do now. Then we returned to our homes to the south, after the harvest. Again, just as many *waubesh* do now. This lands spirit is a summer spirit. At least, that's what some of the Anabe are telling me now. They say that if I lose Tawkenin it will be the spirit of the land reclaiming its true nature. We may have lived here permanently too long. Manitou may will us to leave."

I reflected upon what he said silently. Could this be true? Did Aupetchi really believe it was his destiny to lose the race, to relinquish Tawkenin? The thought was sickening, especially after all I had done. I had created the Anabe's only hope to retain title to their land, and my plan permitted them to do so with great dignity.

"Do you believe this?" I finally asked.

"I do not," he replied. "I believe that when you see a dipper in the night sky, I see a bear. Sometimes we see what we need to see; this helps our spirit find it's true nature. I see that you are giving me the chance to keep our homes. And I see it clearly now because you say you see honor in Cole. Before tonight I had faith it would happen, and now I have hope as well."

I smiled and placed my hand on Aupetchi's. The low rumble of gentle waves accompanied our reflective silences. We both gazed at the lake before us.

"You are right Aupetchi. I have hope too. You know my father used to bring me here, to this beach. We would listen to the waves, feel the breeze, and watch the sky. He told me that whenever he was working, I could find him here. He said he could speak to me through the waves, hold me in the breeze and smile at me from the stars."

I paused for a moment, and then continued.

"Then, suddenly, he disappeared. The lake took him violently and I hated it for that. I was angry and refused to come close to the shore. I vowed to never forgive it for wrecking my father's ship and taking his life. I wanted revenge on the lake, certain it had taken my father purposefully."

Aupetchi nodded solemnly, as if he too felt my anger.

"Not any more, though. Now I again see the lake as a source of hope. I come here and my father speaks to me. I feel his arms around me, protecting me, and I see his eyes sparkle as he looks at me. Eventually I realized that the lake had not changed, had not become vengeful. The only thing that had changed was the way I saw it, the way I felt about it."

I turned to Aupetchi and took his other hand in mine. I looked at him through the darkness.

"Try to see Cole differently, Aupetchi. Believe that he will keep his word, and he will. It really is that simple."

"I will try," Aupetchi said, "for I hear the wisdom in your words."

"Good," I smiled. Then I added, "One more thing: keep training. Cole is working harder than he ever has before and make no mistake, he's a very fast swimmer. Your character will be tested because he very well might win."

"Yes, I know," Aupetchi answered honestly. He understood my point.

COLE

The floodlights of the Greater Detroit Aquatic Center dimmed the brilliance of the evening's stars. In their place, the submerged lights of the swimming pool shimmered through its undulating surface. The refracted light reflected sporadically off the brick facade of the spectator area. The effect was eerie.

The GDAC was old for a competitive swimming pool, built over 20 years earlier by the Works Projects Administration. The pool was 50 meters long, and it had ten lanes and a separate diving well. Many pools claimed to be Olympic sized but most were not; instead they were Olympic shaped, which is to say rectangular. The GDAC was a true Olympic pool, built by the city of Detroit in hopes of hosting the 1936 Olympic Games. It had massive locker rooms and an expansive spectator area. In theory it sat two thousand comfortably, although no crowd that big had ever come. Berlin hosted the games, not Detroit.

The pool's history did not concern me at this time, though. Instead, the peculiar atmosphere I had just entered only added to my distress. I rarely competed outdoors, much less at night in a lighted pool.

Last night I had taken sixth in the 200-meter Freestyle, my worst finish in almost ten years. To add insult to injury, Jay Pond had won the 50-meter Freestyle. In any other year I would have swum the 50 instead of the 200, and would most likely have won. I certainly wouldn't have gotten sixth. But since I was training for college and the Olympics, I had to swim distance. I was now questioning this decision.

Tonight I was scheduled to swim the 400-meter Freestyle. Jay Pond was swimming as well and was favored to win the 100-meter Freestyle. In this meet we would not face each other. This summer that duel would only occur in the waters of Lake Michigan. The 400 was eight times longer than my best sprint race and Olivia wanted me to swim at a set pace. Earlier, during warm-ups, she had huddled next to me and reviewed the race strategy.

"I want you to take out the first 100 in 1:03 or 1:04. Then settle into a 1:10 pace for the next two hundreds. Just continue breathing and keep a good stoke," Olivia said. "Then bring it back as hard as you can, with whatever you have left. Hold your stroke and kick like a kangaroo. A 1:07 final hundred would be great."

"I don't know about that Olivia," I said as I nervously shook out my arms, loosening my triceps. "I can't swim that slow."

"Yes you can, Cole. You can! You've done it in practice, many times, and tonight you'll do it in a race," she said somewhat unconvincingly.

We both knew that she had told me the same thing before the 200.

"Take it out in a minute or a 1:01," she had said then, "then bring it home in a 1:07 or 1:08. If you're *under* 2:10 you should win."

Which proved that Olivia knew her stuff. A 2:10 did win, 2:10.8 to be exact: swum by Timothy Michaels of the Tri-City Swim Club. I had ignored Olivia's advice and sprinted the first hundred, covering the distance in 56.5 seconds, only one second off my all-time best for that distance. Then, when I was a quarter of the way through my second 100 meters, my arms tightened up. My stroke shortened. It became difficult for me to breathe. My legs began to cramp. I struggled through the last 50-meter lap and finished with a time of 2:16.2. I had swum the second 100 meters in 1:19.7. Five swimmers passed me on the last lap. Complicating matters worse was the fact that Gus Wilson, the head coach at Michigan State College, had seen it all. He approached Olivia and me after the race.

"Olivia, congratulations on your college career. Impressive stuff. I only hope Cole can adjust to the longer distances as well as you did," he had said pointedly.

"Coach, I just took it out to fast," I had interjected.

"Indeed Harrison, indeed," Wilson had replied. "Maybe when your sister is your coach that excuse will fly. Just remember that when you get to East Lansing, you're nobody's sister. You'll learn to swim distance."

Thinking about Coach Wilson's comments added to my troubles. I was offended by the disrespect he had shown my sister; Olivia was a good coach. On top of this preoccupation, though, and weighing even more heavily on my mind, was the fact that Kate still hadn't accepted my marriage proposal.

Her initial hesitation hadn't surprised me, but now my patience was wearing thin. The fact that it was still on the table, that she hadn't said no, provided little consolation. I was overwhelmed by the idea that I had to prove so much, to so many people. Even the gift of land my father had given me was proving to be a nuisance rather than a reward, which was so typically Four. And now I was swimming poorly. My future was suddenly in jeopardy, and now it seemed my problems might slow Olivia's aspirations for a coaching career.

She reflected no concern about Gus Wilson's criticism. She ignored his comments and focused her attention upon the job at hand: rebuilding the confidence of her talented athlete, me. Our familiarity and the life we shared enabled her to do just that. Olivia had the key that would unlock my confidence. It was a key that Gus Wilson, despite his good intentions could not have found.

She led me away from the pool, away from the flickering rays and into the starlight. We followed a pathway that led into a metropolitan park adjacent to the swimming complex. In the nearby brush crickets chirped, and in the distance a small nocturnal mammal foraged in the dark. The eerie glow of the pool on the horizon simulated the aurora borealis. The dimmest stars slowly became visible in the clear night sky. Olivia shook out the damp towel she carried with her and placed it on the ground. We sat.

"It's nice out here, isn't it," she began.

"I guess," I mumbled, unmoved by her familiar greeting.

"It reminds me a little of our pier up north," she continued.

The pier at Harbor Point served as our safe haven. When we needed to escape, we sought refuge on the dock. Together we'd look up at the night sky and calm ourselves as the rhythm of the waves beat beneath us.

"I don't think so, Olivia," I argued. "This is nothing like the pier."

"Oh yes it is, in some ways," insisted Olivia. "Look at the stars. If we were sitting on the pier tonight we'd see these same stars. They're with us everywhere we go."

It was only then that I looked up and saw Scorpio and Sagittarius high above us. Immediately I thought of Kate, and our special night in Mackinaw City. Maybe there was something to what Olivia was saying: maybe there was solace in the stars.

"I remember when I was at Skidmore," she continued, "there were times - fortunately not many - but times when I needed to get away. Times when I just wanted to quit; quit swimming, quit studying, quit trying so damn hard."

I adjusted myself on the towel and turned to face her. "I can't imagine you feeling that way. You're always so strong," I offered.

"I know. And that had bothered me too. I knew I shouldn't be so upset, which only disturbed me more."

"I wish I'd have been there for you Olivia. I could have helped."

"I know, and in a way you were," Olivia agreed, "which helped. That's my point."

"But how?" I questioned. "I don't get it."

"Well, when I felt that way I would leave campus to clear my head. About five miles out of town there was a small lake. Well, they called it a lake; we'd call it a pond. But it was water. I'd find an abandoned dock and go sit there, under the night sky, just like we do at the Point. After a while I'd relax, just like I do when I am with you. It was as if you were there with me. Spiritually I think you were. I could sense your presence, comforting me."

I finally smiled. "You know what's weird?" I asked.

"No, what?"

"When you pointed out the stars earlier, I felt like Kate was with me. At least for a just a moment," I said.

"So you know what I mean then," she inferred.

"I guess I do. That's pretty cool. It's like your never alone," I replied.

Olivia gazed knowingly at me, nodding agreement, before continuing. "That's part of it. I felt better then, because I felt your presence. Just like you do now because of Kate's. I also felt safe. That was what helped the most. Knowing that no matter what, you would be there for me. Just like I will always be here for you. That inspired me to go back to campus, get back on whatever horse threw me, and try again."

"And what happened when you did?" I asked.

"I came back stronger and succeeded at whatever I had failed at," she replied.

I leaned back on my elbows and stretched my long legs over the edge of the towel. I instinctively grasped at the cool grass with my toes, as though I was nesting in the northern Michigan sand. I closed my eyes, exhaled deeply, and focused once again upon the stars high above us.

"I see what you're saying and you're right," I acknowledged finally.

"How so?" she asked, hopefully.

"Just because the 200 didn't work out, doesn't mean the 400 won't. I have to go back there and swim my best race."

"That's my take on it," she agreed.

"I was thinking about too much stuff in the 200. My pace, Four, Gus, Kate, you, everything but the race."

"Exactly," Olivia said. "So the question is, how will you swim the 400?"

I thought for a moment before answering. "I want to clear my mind of everything and just focus on my stroke. I don't even want to think about strategy."

"But how can you do that?" she asked.

"The way I figure it is, what I am most of all is a sprinter," I explained. "And as a sprinter what I do best is just swim fast. I don't think, I don't set the pace, I don't develop a strategy, I just get in the water and swim as fast as I can."

"Agreed, but you can't do that in the 400," she declared. "You have to pace yourself."

"No, I don't," I reasoned aloud. "Everyone else in the finals is a distance swimmer, so I'll let one of them set the pace for me."

"Hmm," Olivia mulled this over. "I get it and I like it. Someone like Timothy Michaels, you mean?"

"Perfect," I concluded. "He won't expect a thing after smoking me in the 200."

So we agreed. I wouldn't worry about strategy. I would let Michaels set the pace and stay at his feet for the first 325 meters. Then, I would do what I did best for the last 75 meters: Sprint!

As planned I sprinted past Michaels in the final 75 meters to win the 400 by two body lengths. Afterwards Gus Wilson approached us once again; only this time, he warmly congratulated me. Then he told Olivia about a coaching vacancy he knew of at Albion College.

Less than an hour later I bowed to receive my gold medal. After it was placed around my neck I looked up to the night sky, then found Olivia in the crowd. I nodded to the sky, and then winked at my sister. She smiled and winked back.

Chapter Nine

New Moon

Wednesday, August 23

COLE

My triumphant victory in the 400 at the Water Wonderland filled me with confidence. The Labor Day Race would be mine, I was sure of it now. While preparing for my daily workout I reflected back on the celebration Kate, Olivia and I had enjoyed five nights earlier at Chez Robert.

Kate was tired, but not too tired to share our obvious joy. She knew how important the win was for me. She knew my collegiate and Olympic dreams had moved one step closer to reality. She also knew how important this win had been for Olivia, who had accepted the head coaching position at Albion.

"I can't believe they're going to let you coach the men as well as the women, Olivia," Kate said as she reached for her fifth scallop wrapped in bacon. "That's a real opportunity for you. Are you sure you can do it?"

"Well, Coach Wilson told Albion's President, Dr. W. Harmon Featherstone, that if I could get Cole to win the 400 then I could teach a pig to out-swim a duck," Olivia replied.

"Now that's a race I'd like to see," I added.

"And as for you, Cole," Kate said, redirecting our attention, "I am so proud of you I could just burst. The 400! How did you ever win the 400?"

"Well I don't want to make a habit out of it, that's for sure. It's too long a race for my taste," he answered. "I think I'll stick to the 50 and the 100 in college, with maybe a 200 every now and then. But I know this race did me a lot of good, thanks to Olivia. I'm primed to win the North Country Swim Championship."

"Physically I agree. You are in the best shape ever," Olivia said as she flagged down our tuxedo-clad waiter. "More scallops please."

I had enjoyed this evening more than any other, aside

from the night I proposed to Kate more than a month and a
half ago. My two favorite people in the world were with me,
and they were and lavishing admiration upon me. I was in
a very good place.

Because of that I had thought of pushing my luck and
asking Kate about her current state of matrimonial mind.
Maybe Olivia's presence would weaken her resolve? Plus,
my sister could add a needed and persuasive perspective
that could tilt the balance in my favor. Still I had hesitated.

I knew that one of Kate's strengths was her will. It was
unshakable. I reminded myself that she had not said no;
instead she had said that she loved me, deeply and permanently. To push the issue might have had a negative effect,
pushing her further away rather than drawing her closer.
So had I decided to practice the patience Kate spoke of so
often. Olivia's snapping fingers had returned me to the conversation.

*"I said," Olivia repeated, for my benefit, "that you are
not quite ready yet little brother. You may be primed, but
now we must taper."*

*I blushed. Usually I loved it when she called me little
brother, in private. I found it was an awkward term to hear
in the company of others. Stammering a little, my gaze
shifted lovingly to Kate.*

*"I'm sorry. My mind was wandering to the last time
Kate and I were here," I said.*

Kate took my hand in hers and smiled.

*"That was a wonderful evening, wasn't it?" she an-
swered.*

*I was again tempted to bring up the subject of mar-
riage, but my sister had an agenda of her own.*

*"Really Cole, you have to pay attention. Let this poor
girl sit back and relax. She worked her butt off today and
all you want to do is make goo-goo eyes at her. We need to
talk about your taper, which should start soon."*

And so it did. This was the fourth day of my taper.

Olivia reduced my daily yardage, from over 7,000 to fewer than 4,500. And today, for the first time all summer, I would swim less than 4,000 yards.

Olivia started me off with an 800-yard warm-up, slow and easy. Then I did a set of six descending 500-yard swims. She told me to decrease, or improve, my time by five seconds on each successive swim. She let me rest for a minute and a half between each 500.

Olivia hoped that this would teach me to slowly increase my pace during the open water swim that was now just over a week away. I struggled with the assignment. The first 500 gave me a "base time" which I was to improve upon during the next five. My second and third 500 were each close to ten seconds faster than the previous.

"That's too fast Cole, way too fast," Olivia cautioned.

I stood slightly hunched in the shallow end of the White Pine pool, breathing deeply, my hands on my hips. My eyes avoided Olivia's as I looked off into the distance.

"Come on Olivia, I don't need to work this hard," I exhaled. There's no one up here who can touch me at any distance. Not even Jay Pond, no matter what he thinks. This one's a piece of cake. Let's knock off early and go grab some dinner."

I could tell that Olivia considered my offer. She knew my first three 500s had been exceptionally fast. And I knew she agreed with me: there was no one up north besides Jay Pond that could touch me, and he was a sprinter. On the other hand, she never let me quit early, just as she never quit a workout early. She also knew that the next three 500s were the key to the set. Plus, I knew she was worried about a conversation she had with Kate at our recent dinner together. Olivia had shared the content of this exchange with me just before today's workout. It had happened as we were leaving Chez Robert. I had left the two women alone and went to retrieve my cherished Roadster.

"Olivia?" Kate started, hesitantly.
"Yes Kate?"

"My best friends brother is training for the Labor Day race."

"Oh that's great," Olivia responded supportively. *"I hope he can push Cole for a while so he gets a decent time."*

"Me too. He's been training in the lake all summer long. He even spent close to a month alone on an island near the Straits getting ready for it. I think he swam some-thing like six hours a day."

"Really," Olivia said with much more interest. *"What did you say his name was? Do you know where he swam in high school?"*

"Oh, he didn't go to high school. He's an Anabe, sort of a spiritual chief. His name is Aupetchi. He's Maymegwan's brother," Kate explained. *"What I'm wondering is if you think his never having swum in a pool like Cole will hurt him?"*

"On the contrary," Olivia answered contemplatively. *"In this case I think that might help."*

Before she could explain why I arrived with the Buick and jumped out to let the girls in. I had not noticed that Olivia was deep in thought. Kate had unearthed a weak-ness in her training of me that she had not foreseen. I had never trained in the lake.

I'm sure this memory was in her mind when she quickly decided that I must finish the set at hand.

"You know the rules little brother. We eat after we workout. Now let's get going, you've already doubled your rest, you lazy bum," Olivia directed.

"All right Olivia, I'm gone," I replied before pushing off the wall of the pool.

My next three 500s were slower than my last and barely faster than my first. My inability to descend any of the final three 500s only added to Olivia's growing angst.

"Cole, you've got to learn to descend all five, not just two," she urged. "You're second and third were just too fast. If anyone manages to stay with you for the first mile and a half you could lose."

"As if, sis. No one here can touch me I tell you," I replied confidently.

"Hmm, seems like I remember General Custer expressing the same sentiment," Olivia reminded me.

Olivia's reference bothered me. I looked at her quizzically. The image of the troublesome stone carver came to my head. I suspected Aupetchi might be able to hang on my heels; after all he did swim distance. I knew that much about him. The question was, could he stay with m for the last few yards of the race?

"Good point Olivia," I answered, suddenly sharing my sister's uneasiness, "good point."

KATE

Maymegwan and I had plans for this day so I woke early, at five a.m. After dressing quickly I drove to Tawkenin, picked her up and headed to Mackinaw City. During the drive I thought back to the evening I had shared with Cole and Olivia at Chez Robert. Conflicting emotions raced through my mind.

On the plus side, I could still see Cole taking my hand, reminding me of the evening he proposed. At that moment I had felt closer to him than ever before. As we clasped hands I had been overwhelmed by a desire to protect him. His firm grasp and pleading gaze communicated his need for my unconditional love, a look I had rarely seen this summer. A need he had not communicated to me since our first visit to Chez Robert.

But there was a negative side too. Olivia's apprehension about Cole's mental state had concerned me. We all knew that self-confidence was one of Cole's greatest gifts; however if Olivia was right and Cole was too confident, he might be blind to the challenge before him. I knew Aupetchi would be a formidable opponent. He would test Cole's character as it had never been tested before.

And to make matters worse I learned that Olivia had shared her concern about his preparedness with Four. Needless to say, Four was displeased, which infected the entire Harrison home. I understood how this affected Cole. He wasn't troubled because his father was concerned about his lack of focus; he was always concerned about something. He was disturbed because the news had aborted the accolades he sought after his win at the Water Wonderland. Accolades that for him were few and far between. Two days after our dinner at Chez Robert I had tried to console Cole.

I woke early and went to the Summit Street Bakery, perched on a bluff overlooking the waterfront. It was one of my favorite breakfast stops. I bought a half a dozen fresh baked donuts and filled my thermos with piping hot coffee.

Then I drove down State Street to Bay. Turning right I traveled the short distance to Traverse Street, which led to the gated entrance of Harbor Point.

I knew the guard well. His name was Victor Marichal and his brother was in my grade at school. Victor had graduated two years earlier. His family first came to the area as migrant workers from Mexico, helping collect the cherry harvest. They settled permanently in the area seven years ago and had attended my church ever since. Victor waved me through, after I made him promise to not announce my arrival to the Harrison home as he was paid to do. He agreed easily to honor the code of the locals: take care of our own first.

I arrived unnoticed at the massive cottage via the service road, and parked by the kitchen door. It was just before breakfast and I could see Bradford and the cook preparing for the meal. I walked to the screen door and asked Bradford if he would tell Cole and Olivia to meet me on the dock. He agreed to do so, and a few moments later they arrived. Cole greeted me affectionately.

"What a great way to start the day, Kate!" he gushed as he hugged me tightly.

"Yes," Olivia added cautiously, "this is quite a surprise. Our parents are beside themselves."

I looked back to the house and saw the silhouettes of Four and Elizabeth on the landscaped verandah. They were trying to be discreet but I knew they were looking suspiciously at the three of us, now comfortably seated on the dock.

Cole's tanned legs hung over the docks edge, swinging rhythmically. Olivia stretched hers out on the dock, and leaned back to let the morning sun hit her face. Both wore khaki shorts, brown docksiders, and open collared polo shirts: Cole's green, Olivia's pink. I was clad in light blue clam diggers and a sleeveless white blouse. I wore navy Ked's sneakers without socks. Our difference in class was obvious, and I had to smile to myself.

"Isn't it a beautiful morning?" I began.

"Looks to be," Cole agreed as he scanned the eastern horizon.

Olivia said nothing. I did not push. I knew that the relationship between brother and sister, athlete and coach was strained. I knew Cole believed Olivia had forsaken him. He felt it was wrong of her to tell their parents her concern. He felt Olivia had overstepped her duty as his coach and betrayed his confidence. Olivia had failed him as his sister for the first time. I was sure Olivia knew how he felt. I also knew Olivia had never meant to hurt him, so I continued despite the tension.

"I got you each coffee. Light cream and sugar for Olivia, black for Cole."

"Very thoughtful," Olivia offered.

"Thanks," I said while looking at Olivia warmly. "I also brought two creme filled donuts for you."

"Raspberry creme," Olivia noted, "yummy. Did you know that they're my favorite?"

"Of course I did. Cole told me," I replied. "He talks about you all the time. I feel like I know everything about you, your greatest achievements and your silliest habits."

Olivia looked at Cole and smiled a hopeful little half-smile. Cole ignored her.

"And for you Master Harrison, one cinnamon twist and one chocolate frosted donut," I continued.

"Thanks Kate," he said. "Now why don't you tell us what this is all about."

"I think I can help with that," Olivia interjected.

"I'm sure you can. You're always ready to speak up, aren't you Olivia? You always have something to say," Cole said sarcastically.

"About you, yes. You bet I do," Olivia answered, "and I won't apologize for caring about you and loving you and wanting what is best for you. Someone in this family has to give that to you."

"So that's how it is then. You just fill the void because you have to?" Cole glared.

"Cole, that's not fair," I interrupted. "You've told me

many times that Olivia's always been, above all else, your friend."

"That's right Cole," Olivia added. "I remember the day mother brought you home. I was so anxious to have a brother, to have a friend. It was a dreary childhood until you arrived. I looked into your eyes and knew my prayers had been answered. I still believe that. I've always believed that."

Cole's legs stopped rocking and he sat very still. He took a sip of coffee. Small waves rolled beneath us while I lightly massaged the back of his neck.

"Olivia didn't mean to hurt you," I said.

"It's true Cole," Olivia added, "you know how father is. He just kept pressing me about how your training was coming. I told him that your win in Detroit was your best race ever and how I was so proud of you. I told him I hoped he and mother would tell you how proud they were. He just ignored me. All he wanted to hear about was Labor Day and the Olympics. All I said was that you're certain you'll win next week. He asked me if I agreed and I said I was a little more nervous than you were. That's all, a little more nervous."

She paused to take a sip of her beverage.

"Four thought that meant you were overconfident," she continued. "He has to find something about you to improve. He always has. I am genuinely sorry Cole. I should have known he'd take it all the wrong way. I just wanted them to know what a great job you did in the Water Wonderland."

Cole remained silent. He rolled his head to facilitate my massage. Then he cleared his throat, took a bite out of his donut and another swig of coffee, and turned to Olivia.

"I'll trade you half of my cinnamon twist for a bite of your raspberry cream."

Olivia embraced her younger brother and wiped a tear from her eye. The rift was healed. After we devoured the donuts and drained the coffee I left the siblings so they could continue the training.

I smiled inwardly at this memory as Maymegwan and I boarded an Arnold Line ferry in Mackinaw City. It was just after eight a.m. After tentatively working our way through a thick early-morning fog that masked the vessel, we found seats on the open-air upper deck. I intended to relax today, since the next few weeks would be the most important in the White Pine's summer season.

◆◆◆

Two critical objectives had to be accomplished in the half month remaining until Labor Day weekend. First, and most obvious, the White Pine had to capture as much gross revenue as possible. We typically made close to twenty percent of our annual income in this two-week period. Every able body and capable mind had to be on the floor. No one took vacation or got multiple days off during the last stretch, ever.

The second objective defined the White Pine's business philosophy. We worked towards it each and every day, all summer long. My mother originally recognized the phenomenon and wisely made it the restaurants primary goal. She called it the "transformation" and it guaranteed the continued success of the White Pine.

She had first seen it occur three years earlier and immediately recognized its potential. That summer had been my first as lunch supervisor. I had inherited a small customer core of aging regulars, and by the end of the summer a lively lunch trade surrounded this nucleus.

Word of mouth fueled the curiosity of fudgies and inquisitive locals, and new customers continually flocked through our rough-hewn doors. From their first moment inside, our magic overpowered them. The fudgies became faithful immediately, often returning for dinner the very same day. These loyal summer residents were the cornerstones of a successful business in Harbor Springs. Yet what truly distinguished us was our knack for hooking the curious locals. Like the fudgies they would experiment with a casual lunch, like it, and return for dinner. The dinner atmosphere created by my mother always hooked them. Be it local or fudgie: dinner transformed them into regulars.

My mother created a sociable and personable environment at dinner that was the envy of the entire northeast Michigan coast, from Ludington to Mackinaw City. Our service staff was friendly and attentive while production was timely and consistently superior. By their third visit, my mother would greet customers by name. On any given evening the lounge had the familiar feel of a family reunion. The warmth of the room was comforting, intoxicating and addictive.

This summer's transformation was almost complete. For the past month every day had been busier than the day before, a trend that would continue until Labor Day. I needed this day off.

No sooner had we gotten to our seats than the ferry departed. The wind picked up as we moved into the Straits. May and I were headed to Mackinac Island, where we would spend the day riding horses, eating fudge and shopping.

We huddled together on the deck, bracing against the wind. We could have gone below, into the enclosed cabin, for the thirty-minute ride. We decided against it. Too many fudgies were gathered there already, despite the early hour. As we approached the harbor the fog finally lifted. May and I gathered our belongings and peered forward through the intermittent spray. The ferry's bow cut into medium-sized swells. When we were just outside the breakwater we studied our island destination.

"There it is," I said, "the great turtle, Michilimackinac."

"We Anabe call it Mishinemackinawgo," said May.

"Really?" I asked. "I was always told that Michilimackinac was an accurate Anabe translation."

"Like many so-called Indian legends that is not what

we were taught," May continued. "Michilimackinac is an inaccurate translation that has a false legend built around it."

"Oh come on May, I think you're pulling my leg. I was told that's why there's a difference in the spelling, Mackinac and Mackinaw. One is the *waubesh* spelling and one is the authentic Anabe term. Everyone knows that."

"In the *waubesh* world perhaps," May agreed, "and it has nothing to do with a turtle. That is a different legend altogether."

"Tell me more, May. What is it if not a turtle," I probed, "and how did the name Michilimackinac become so well accepted?"

"First of all, if the Anabe were to call the island a great turtle we would say *mikinock* for turtle and *mishe* for tremendous in size. Put them together and we would say *mishemikinock*, or monstrous turtle," May explained.

"I see," I said thoughtfully. "So the early *couriers de bois* mistook the phrase *mishinemackinawgo* for *mishemikinock*."

"So it seems. Although the island does look a little like a turtle, my people can see this too," May replied.

We paused as the ferry slowed to round the breakwater. The fudgies who crossed the Straights in the below cabin emerged, ascending onto the open-air deck. We all admired the island view. What had been a barely visible silhouette at the start of our journey was now a well-defined shoreline. The massively beautiful Grand Hotel, with the world's longest porch, stood majestically on a bluff to our left. The breakwater branched out and away from the small downtown skyline, if the term skyline could be applied to a historic commercial strip whose largest building was a four-story hotel built of white pine.

We moved aft to avoid the fudgies huddled on the bow as the boat passed through the main shipping channel. From the stern we looked behind us and watched a seven hundred-foot freighter move slowly away from us. Its foghorn bellowed periodically, announcing her purposeful progress. As the ferry turned to enter the harbor the Round Island lighthouse came into view. May continued.

"Kate, we have known each for many years. I know that you, unlike most *waubesh*, have come to understand my people. With all that you know about us do you really believe that a spiritual place such as *mishinemackinawgo* would be named after a mud turtle?" she asked.

"Well when you put it that way, maybe not. It isn't consistent with all that I've learned about the Anabe," I replied. "It does seem too simple, too European, to be the true legend. I guess I just accepted the story because I had heard it so much."

"Yes, it is easy to believe what we often hear, even if it is false," May reasoned. "The truth is sometimes hard to divine. However, I know the true tradition of this island."

"So tell me about it already. The suspense is killing me," I teased.

"When the Anabe first came to Mackinac, as you call it, it was already inhabited," May began. "This was long before the *waubesh* first arrived. We approached the island to trade with the people living here. The island people called themselves *mishinemackinawgo*. We soon learned that the *mishinemackinawgo* feared a terrible enemy, whom they called *nodowa*."

"Who where these *nodowa*?" I interrupted, "I have never heard of such a nation."

As we spoke a few passengers moved close, subtly eavesdropping on our conversation. May did not seem to notice. If she did she was not offended by their encroach-ment. Instead, she increased her volume just a little.

"You have not, for *nodowa* was not the name of the people. It was a term of repugnance. There once were five nations who became one. We knew them as *haudenosau-nee*; the *waubesh* called them Iroquois. *Nodowa* was the *mishinemackinawgo* term for snake, for that is what they considered them."

"I see," I replied. "Please go on."

"One winter a *nodowa* war party visited the island and

annihilated the *mishinemackinawgo*. Only two people escaped the brutality: a strong boy and a brave girl. Each had
seen fourteen winters. They were lovers. The pair slipped
away in the long night."

"How did they escape?" I asked.

"When the warriors arrived the lovers hid in one of the
island's many caves. From this sanctuary they heard the
invading *nodowa* slithering towards the village. They
feared the worst, so they stayed in the cave throughout the
ordeal. When the invaders finally retreated from the island,
the lovers cautiously left their sanctum. The carnage they
discovered convinced them to leave immediately and forever. Naturally cautious and understandably fearful, they
devised a plan of escape."

The ferry surged as the captain reversed engines and
backed the vessel into the dock. A small crowd of local
workers waited on the pier for their daily supplies arriving
from the mainland. By mid-afternoon they would be replaced by tired fudgies anxious to return to Mackinaw City
and their automobiles. As the deckhands tied up the boat,
May continued. We remained in the stern, surrounded by a
small, attentive crowd.

"To avoid detection, the lovers inverted the direction
of their snowshoes and crossed the frozen lake. This tactic
convinced the *nodowa* that the tracks they found were
from people going to the island, not leaving it. The couple
successfully escaped and disappeared into the forests of
the Lower Peninsula. Ever since then the people that had
known the *mishinemackinawgo* best, the people who had
traded with them, met in this area for years to come.
These people were the members of the Fire Nations, what
you call the Anabe, Ojibwa, and Potowatomi. We have
called the island Mishinemackinawgo ever since."

The group of passengers gathered around us numbered
about twenty, each listening intently to May's compelling
story. I was the most avid listener. May paused for a moment, permitting me to absorb all I had been told. Slowly
the crowd dispersed, thinking May was finished. The pas-

sengers congregated around the gangway. Only May and I remained aft.

"That's a sad story Maymegwan, much too poignant to be revered by the Europeans," I said reflectively. "But I wonder what ever happened to the lovers? They experienced so much heartache together, I hope they found happiness after their escape."

"Oh they did, my friend. In fact we believe their spirit exists even today. We call it *pawgishnawboy*," May said. "The massacre disgusted them so they avoid creatures of the Surface World. Instead they exist only in the deepest, most remote woods."

"I bet they are still deeply in love. It's reassuring in a way."

"Yes, I believe that too," May said. "Legend says that they still remain in the wild country, seen or unseen, whichever they choose. Even now, when the Anabe travel in the wild country we hear them in the shadows. Sometimes they sneak into our camps and make our dogs bark or they throw rocks at our *wigwoms*. At times they have even shown themselves to an Anabe, which is a great honor. That witness is seen as prophet and believed to possess great wisdom. Sawmay himself is said to have spoken with *pawgishnawboy*. This is one reason he is so revered and why his support of Aupetchi's swim is so valued. We sense *pawgishnawboy* watching him from the shadows, and believe that Aupetchi will be protected."

"How beautiful," I said. "You know, I've seen Aupetchi on the beach a few times this summer and I have always sensed that he was not alone. That he was being watched, no - make that protected - by someone or something I could not see."

"This does not surprise me. Did this frighten you?" May asked.

"No. In fact I felt comforted by it. Weird, isn't it?"

"Not at all. *Pawgishnawboy* can watch many people and influence many lives at the same time. They are very benevolent. Perhaps because they were lovers themselves they are watching over you and Cole," May suggested.

"Do you really think so? That would be so wonderful," I exclaimed.

The ferry was moored and almost empty by the time we finished. After one last look over the water across the Straits, we disembarked to start our day on Mishinemacki-nawgo.

AUPETCHI

Only eight days remained before the most important day of my young life: the day that would determine the future of my people. The Anabe were extremely confident in me because they knew I was physically prepared. I had never been in better shape. Furthermore the Anabe knew of Sawmay's vision. They knew that the spirit of muskrat and the power of Manitou were with me. My quest was blessed.

The most spiritual band of the Anabe said I was *nebawbawyew*, or "filled with spiritual power." The future of Tawkenin, the north and south villages, the Michi Gama shoreline that ran between them and all the land that surrounded them seemed secure. I would win the race; of this the elders and wise men were certain.

However, virtually every elder and wise man could recall a time when they had been as certain of different outcomes, all of which never materialized. They all knew promises could be broken, that apparent success could become failure. So after much discussion and at the urging of one particular tribunal, the Midewin, it was agreed that I should renew my spiritual force before the race.

The members of the Midewin were the Anabe medicine people. The Anabe often deferred to the wishes of these revered men and women, called *mide*. The people believed that Manitou gave the *mide* a rare gift: the power to heal. They were a wise and gifted group who promoted good health through balanced living, herbal medicine, and ceremonial ritual.

The Midewin invited me to partake in a different, rarely used, ritual. They felt I needed to seek support from the ruling demon of the Under Water World, the notorious and elusive Black Panther. Proof of the Black Panther's existence could be seen in every lake and river, as he diabolically created powerful whirlpools and wild rapids from his lair.

It was this power that the Midewin hoped to appease in

the ceremony they had summoned me to on this day. They wanted me to find the water surface accommodating during my upcoming race. They wanted the Black Panther to be still. And so I was invited into the *midewigaan,* or medicine lodge.

The medicine lodge's frame was made of live sapling and covered by strips of birch bark. It had two doors. The light of every sunrise could be seen through the eastern door, the light of every sunset through the western. An opening in the ceiling let smoke from a small fire escape and find its way to Manitou.

I entered the medicine lodge through the eastern door and was met by Sawmay and four *mide* who sat around the perimeter of the lodge, drumming rhythmically. They asked me to sit and I did. Sawmay lit a clay pipe sculpted into a panther effigy and each of us smoked from it. When we were finished, four figures representing the four directions came in and began to dance around the fire. Then figures symbolizing the Sky and Surface worlds danced into the lodge. The *mide* instructed me to rise and join them, so I did, mimicking their moves.

I moved first on one foot, then on the other. I bowed my head and slouched my shoulders, mumbling gutturally, barely audible. Every few minutes I spun feverishly and threw my hands to the sky wildly, arching my back and stretching my neck. I cried out loudly, repeating the phrases I had muttered just moments ago.

Finally, after more than an hour of this, we were joined by four new figures, each representing one of the many moods of the Panther. They symbolized power, stealth, grace, and speed. Their attention was clearly focused upon me, although they pestered the entire circle. Soon Sky World, Surface World, and the four directions retreated into the shadows of the *midewigaan.*

I slowed to an imperceptible shuffle. My head was bowed and my eyes closed. The *mide* drummers slowed the rhythm and decreased the power of their beat. The fire

cracked sporadically, contributing sound, light and aroma
to the atmosphere of the lodge.

Suddenly, an elaborate and colorful image burst into
the *midewigaan* from the western door. The figure had the
head of a thunderbird and the body of a man. It was covered in animal robes from head to toe. It carried a scepter-
like object adorned with sacred eagle feathers. The only
sound in the lodge was the crackle of the fire. This was
Kenwagun, one the most revered ancestors of the Anabe.

The beat of the drum grew louder and stronger. Wood
was added to the fire, igniting its roar. The four directions
re-emerged, dancing confidently. Black panther stood defensively in the middle of the growing dance circle. Panther
eyed the crowd cautiously. Kenwagun drew a *megis*, or sacred shell, from his robe. He took the *megis* and
ritualistically shot Black Panther. Panther fell to the floor,
and seemed to fall asleep. Sky and Surface World rejoined
the dance circle. The smell of sweetgrass permeated the
lodge.

The dancers continued their frenetic pace while I maintained my slow shuffle. Finally, almost an hour later,
Panther stirred from his sleep. He groomed himself,
stretched and looked about him. The four figures representing Black Panther left, then returned quickly, except they
now showed him to be benevolent, open, gentle, and pa-
tient. The spirit of Panther had been reborn and he started
dancing with the others.

I increased my pace. I picked up my feet and lifted my
knees. My eyes snapped open and my head darted from
side to side. My arms and torso began to swing and twist. I
joined the circle with Panther dancing behind me, and
moved with the group effortlessly and unmolested.

This continued well into the morning, until only I remained dancing. Finally the Midewin and Sawmay left me
alone in the lodge. The ceremony had ended. The ritual was
completed. My journey through the lair of the Panther
would be safe. Still, I continued to move slowly around the
fire.

Finally I stopped, banked the fire, and left the medicine lodge. I covered the doors with deerskin flaps and walked towards the water. I entered Michi Gama, the monster lake, and bathed in her fresh, clean water. Devoutly I thanked Manitou for the new day and for the service he was about to perform for my people. I submerged myself in the traditional manner and swam easily and slowly, at the same pace at which I had been dancing earlier, for one and a half hours. Then I returned to my *wigwom* and slept for fifteen hours. I was exhausted.

Chapter Ten

WAXING QUARTER

Friday, September 1

KATE

Excitement filled the air as the sun rose over Harbor Springs, marking the first day of the Harbor Festival. The long weekend would end as it always did, with a gala fireworks display over Little Traverse Bay. Traditional festival activities would fill the three days leading up to this finale; however, this year the new opening event added fervor to the usual commotion. That event was the open water swim race.

A small crowd arrived early on the shores of Bay View, a Methodist summer retreat across Little Traverse Bay. Bay View would serve as the starting point. The race would finish at the public dock in Harbor Springs. Organizers were certain that Cole Harrison would be the winner and hoped to capitalize on his local ties, as did I.

I had come up with a creative way to profit from the race. To implement my plan my mother and I needed all the time we could get, so we had gotten up two hours before sunrise to begin our preparations. It was now midmorning and we could hear the clatter of carnival rides being erected in City Park, three blocks away. Food vendors upwind of us filled the air with the alluring odor of dough frying, sausage grilling, and fresh peppers and onions sautéing. Craftspeople bustled about, assembling their displays. The festival would start in less than an hour.

Festival organizers calculated that it would take Cole about an hour and a half to finish the swim. The opening ceremonies were scheduled around this estimate. The race would start at 11:30 a.m., across the bay. Opening ceremonies in Harbor Springs were scheduled for noon. Local dignitaries would speak for an hour, at which time Cole would appear on the horizon. Then the local hero would round Harbor Point and head to the finish line accompanied by the tumultuous clamor of the crowd. At least, that was the plan.

Cole's father had persuaded the festival sponsors to
route the swimmers directly in front of his cottage, just
before they finished at the public beach. Consequently,
Four and Elizabeth were now entertaining seventy-two
guests with a pre-race champagne brunch.

The public beach was adjacent to the White Pine Inn,
a fact that piqued my entrepreneurial nature. Knowing
the beach would be packed for the race I told my mother
that this would present a golden opportunity for us.
Mother disagreed, assuring me that only stragglers would
wander over to the White Pine. Few would want to miss
Cole's heroics and the rest would feast upon the offerings
being cooked in City Park. She felt we should give our
staff a much-needed day off and close the restaurant. I
disagreed, suggesting that if the people wouldn't come to
the Inn, the Inn should go to the people. My idea was to
sell White Pine food at the beach.

After much persuasion, mother agreed to try it. The
concept was simple: we'd sell boxed lunches and cold bev-
erages to the crowd on the beach. Only a skeleton crew
would remain at the Inn; the rest would prepare, pack,
and sell to the throng. Mother remained skeptical but I
think she wanted to reward my initiative. The clincher
was a box I had made up in advance, adorned with a dis-
tinctive new emblem I had created.

The emblem was a circle bordering the silhouette of
twin pine trees and the outline of a welcoming front porch
and a small flock of gulls. An orange iridescent sun set
behind the trees. The White Pine Inn's name was discretely displayed below the image.

I explained to mother that this could be our very own
logo. I told her that we could use the logo on more than
just the boxes. I suggested napkins, flatware, and
matches as a start. Mother loved the idea and agreed to
test the boxes and the logo today.

The morning was misty when we awoke, but had now
given way to a cloudless sky and a comfortable 70-degree

day. We had set up four eight-foot tables into a flattened U shape. We would sell the boxed lunches over the front two, offering two choices.

One included homemade potato salad, fresh cut crudities, two large chocolate chip cookies, a large dill pickle, carrot raisin slaw, a slice of smoked chub, and a prime rib sandwich served with sharp cheddar, a dab of horseradish, lettuce and sweet Bermuda onion on an Kaiser roll. The other lunch was identical except that the sandwich was served on an onion roll and consisted of roast wild turkey, Muenster cheese, the White Pine's unique mayonnaise-mustard seed spread, lettuce, and a ripe Emmet County tomato slice.

We had made three hundred of each, and would make close to a dollar profit on every sale. We had placed iced bottles of pop and beer behind us, under the shade of a benevolent elm tree that bordered the beach. A variety of condiments were available along the two side tables, as were napkins, paper cups, and trash receptacles. We were ready.

I took a moment before the crowd arrived and walked to the shore. I looked wistfully across the water and located the city of Petoskey. I shifted my view eastward along the shore until I could make out the faint outline of the Bay View Inn. I was too far away to see any human activity, yet in my mind I could see Cole engaged in his pre-race routine. I prayed that he was ready too, for whatever fortune the day brought him. Without thinking I found myself praying for Aupetchi as well.

COLE

My routine never varied; regardless of circumstance, location, or emotion, the drill was always the same. Olivia and I had developed independent yet strikingly similar routines when we first began swimming competitively over ten years ago. At first it was just a game we played together, a variation of follow the leader. As we matured, we each put a personal spin on the classic Harrison routine. Mine had remained constant for the past three years, for over two hundred races.

I had gone to bed at nine o'clock last night after a dinner of grilled sirloin steak, baked potato, fresh steamed green beans, and a large hot fudge sundae. This was my traditional "night before" training meal. The menu was similar to the meals I ate at the Western Reserve Academy, would eat at Michigan State College, and those that I hoped to eat at the Olympic Village in Helsinki. The only unusual personal variation was the hot fudge sundae.

That part had been added a decade earlier when Olivia and I were restless the night before our first foray into competitive swimming. The Birmingham Country Club had begun an age-group program at Four's urging and we were members of the original squad. We were both reluctant participants. After dinner the night before our first meet we retreated into the comfortable company of our nanny, Loretta. She lovingly calmed our nerves and sent us to bed satiated by a hot fudge sundae, served without Four's knowledge and contrary to his wishes. Thus a tradition was born.

Last night's sundae did the trick. I fell asleep quickly, seemingly unaffected by the concern surrounding the race. Olivia woke me at 6:30 a.m. and her behavior did not betray the fact that this was the biggest day of my life. We enjoyed a breakfast of plain boiled spaghetti topped with a little melted butter, at my urging. Olivia had vehemently argued with me about this breakfast preference all summer long. She had just recently bent to my whim, only after I had reasoned with her.

I explained that I had added this tradition three years ago while at the Western Reserve Academy. I was an unimpressive sophomore recovering from a mild bout of the flu, and most foods were presenting a bit of a challenge to my system. The Academy's cook recommended this alternative as a means of ensuring that I keep my breakfast down. I digested the spaghetti easily, especially without the acidic tomato sauce. Then I swept my two sprint events to lead our underdog Academy team to an upset win over the Gilmour School, a perennial swimming powerhouse. I had been virtually unstoppable ever since that day, winning my final twenty-seven consecutive dual meet races. I couldn't explain why it helped; I just knew that it did. Olivia couldn't argue with the logic so she acquiesced.

After breakfast I returned to my large bedroom overlooking the lake. I closed the door and turned on my RCA hi-fi, where two long-playing records waited for me. First the Glenn Miller Orchestra swung while I lathered up, unfolded a straight razor and carefully removed the hair from my face, arms, legs, and chest. Then, while Count Basie pounded out a lively rhythm, I closed my eyes and sat very still. Most of the time the Count inspired me to tap my feet or drum my fingers. However, before a race, I concentrated on keeping the energy within me; I knew I might need it later. Instead I imagined myself swimming the race: methodically, purposefully, and victoriously.

I stayed in my room until the race was two hours away. Then Olivia came and gently tapped on my door. I did not respond. She repeated her tapping, louder this time. I greeted her with silence once again. She followed her third attempt with a statement.

"It's time little brother."

Finally, I opened the door. I wore forest green cotton

pants, a gray sweatshirt that read *Reserve Swimming*, no socks and leather sandals. In my hand I carried a green terrycloth towel.

"It is indeed big sister," I replied as I strode past Olivia and moved quickly down the ornately carved front staircase.

My parents saw me descend and excused themselves from the brunch crowd milling about on the garden patio. They met me at the front door. My mother clasped her hands around mine and reached over to kiss each cheek.

"Good luck son," she said encouragingly.

"Thank you, mother."

My mother held the embrace for a moment, which surprised me. Then she released her grip. I moved away to approach Four; Olivia and mother stepped away together.

"Watch over him Olivia, won't you please," Elizabeth urged.

"I will mother. And please do me a favor as well," Olivia responded. "I believe Cole will win, and we all know he should win, but there is a chance that he won't. Jay Pond is swimming, as is Aupetchi, Maymegwan's brother. This will be a tough race for Cole, especially in the turbulent lake water."

"I know that dear," Elizabeth answered.

"Good. Because I think that if he does swim well he should be welcomed back home as a champion, regardless of the outcome."

"Oh Olivia, you know I will do just that," Elizabeth said definitively.

"Yes I do mother, but it's not you I'm worried about," Olivia replied pointedly." It's not you at all."

"I'll do what I can dear," Elizabeth promised honestly. "Now you go along and help him win. That will be best for all of us."

Meanwhile, Four had escorted me off to the spacious front porch, to a private area far from the crowd.

"Cole, I can't remember when I have looked forward to a day as much as I have this one," he began. "Every father hopes that his son will exceed his own achievements."

"I don't think I could do that father," I answered while silently promising myself otherwise. I knew Four preferred deference to arrogance in his children.

"Perhaps not son, but then I never felt I had matched my father's achievements either," Four revealed. "But that's not my point."

This rare crack in my father's evasive demeanor startled and momentarily silenced me. He continued either unaware or unconcerned by my reaction.

"My point is that it is not the quality of the achievement, it is the quality of the effort that is important."

"So you're saying you appreciate the work I've done to prepare for today?" I probed.

"No, not exactly, although I know you are diligent in your preparation, much like your sister," Four replied. "I am saying that when you win you will have achieved more in one day than I have in any single year because you will have earned it with your sweat."

Four grabbed me by both shoulders, turned to me and looked directly into my eyes. I met his stare.

"You were born a winner, Cole. Always remember that. A winner who can begin to build his name, his future and his riches in less than two hours." Four instructed. Then added, "Show no mercy."

Four then dismissed me. The brunch crowd wished us success. I asked Olivia to drive my Roadster, so she chauffeured me to the Bay View Inn.

A small crowd of well wishers greeted us and offered further encouragement as we exited the car and strode purposefully to the starting line on the adjacent beach. It was encouragement that only Olivia heard.

"This is the one, Harrison."

"Good luck Cole."

"Remember Kate's waiting for you at the finish line."

I heard nothing. I was focused completely upon the race at hand. I isolated myself from the crowd and moved towards the shoreline where I stretched and methodically disrobed alongside the other competitors. The start was minutes away. Olivia joined me, collecting my clothes and wishing me luck.

"This is it little brother," she coached. "Remember to swim smart and let Jay Pond do the work. Let him set the pace just like Timothy Michaels did in Detroit."

"I will, coach," I smiled. "I'll hang back until we round the point. Then he can eat my wake."

"That's the plan," Olivia agreed.

She leaned over and gave me a kiss on the cheek. Jay Pond, standing a couple of yards away, laughed.

"How about one of those for me Olivia?" he teased.

"I don't think so Jay," Olivia said with disgust.

"Oh come on Harrison, I'll even slip you a little," he continued, wagging his tongue in her direction.

"She doesn't waste time with losers, Pond Scum," I interjected.

"Then why is she hanging out with you?" Jay replied.

Olivia moved away from Jay and I followed her. She stopped and whispered into my ear.

"Forget it Cole, and remember to stay on his heels. Let him set the pace."

"Don't worry, he can't get to me. He's only wasting his breath trying to psyche me out. I am ready to go," I said confidently.

"That's the way. Now get down to the starting line, I think you're about to go."

I walked to the congested starting area as directed. Then I stopped, shook my arms to relax my muscles, bent over and stretched my legs one more time. I took five deep breaths. I was ready.

The large number of race participants surprised me. All age groups, from eight upwards, would start simultaneously. Young and old mingled together near the starting line: over150 swimmers in all, each absorbed in their personal pre-race ritual. I worked my way to the front of the crowd. I did not want my start slowed by amateurs.

Jay Pond emerged through the throng and grabbed me by my shoulders.

"Good luck Harrison," he said, "although you'll need more than that to stay with me."

I did not reply, nor did I acknowledge Jay's presence. Neither did I notice that Aupetchi had positioned himself to my left, slightly behind me. I focused solely upon the task at hand.

The starter asked for silence. The race was about to begin. Jay, Aupetchi and I moved constantly, working for an edge, always remaining close to one another. We each understood that this was our race. The multitude behind us was meaningless, more of a nuisance than a concern.

"Quiet for the start please, quiet for the start," the judge shouted.

The crowd grudgingly obliged.

"Swimmers, take your mark," the announcer commanded over a few persistent murmurs.

The mob of racers became motionless as each competitor stood at the ready, prepared to run twenty yards across the sandy beach into the cool blue lake. Jay, Aupetchi and I each intended to reach the water first. Quiet anticipation filled the air.

Bang.

The starting pistol's fire broke the silence, followed immediately by shouts of encouragement. At the sound of the blast the three of us broke into a full run. When we reached the surf Jay surged to an early lead by taking exaggerated high steps, clearing the waterline easily with each stride. His lifeguard training served him well.

I mimicked his motion. Olivia had planned for this. I was on Jay's heels when we dove into the water, thirty feet from shore. Accustomed to ritualistic entries into the sacred water, Aupetchi was far behind us, slowed by two-dozen swimmers who had outrun him.

Jay retained the lead as we pulled away from shore and moved past the first buoy, a half-mile out. I followed closely behind him, swimming one body length behind him with Pond's kicking feet in sight. This is where I would swim most of the race, on Jay Pond's heels, waiting to explode when we rounded the Point and approached the finish. Unbeknownst to me, the U.S. Life Savings Corps' annual competition made Jay very familiar with this tactic, so Jay purposefully slowed his rhythm. Aupetchi, still battling through the throng ahead of him, was forty seconds behind.

Jay's strategy went unnoticed. I did not realize that Jay was swimming slowly purposefully. I did not know that I was inadvertently permitting Jay to conserve his energy for the final sprint. Because I was not pushing the pace, Jay might be able to conserve enough energy to hold off my final surge. The texture of the race was changing and I did not know it. Only Jay Pond knew, and ironically, only Aupetchi would benefit.

Still I swam confidently, certain that Aupetchi posed a hollow threat, as I could see no one behind me. It seemed that my only competition was Jay Pond. The two of us swam synchronously as we passed the one-mile buoy. Meanwhile, Aupetchi had maneuvered his way through the throng in front of him and quietly moved into third place. He was only fifteen seconds behind us, and two-thirds of the race remained.

AUPETCHI

I swam as if in a hypnotic trance, oblivious to my sur‐
roundings. My kick was strong and rhythmic, and my
unique swimming style proved to be particularly effective
in the swells of the open lake. My ancestry had prepared
me for this day physically; Anabe ritual had primed me
mentally. Because we never formally raced in the water,
history told us of no great Anabe aquatic competitor. Our
most revered swimmer was Audekawmeg, who was ad‐
mired for his endurance and stamina, not his speed.
Consequently I was creating a new legend with every
stroke, and had since the moment I awoke this morning.

◆◆◆

Last night I had slept on Bliss Beach, tucked into a
protective valley among the sand dunes near Kate's home.
Sawmay escorted me there and left me in solitude. He
understood that my fate was now in Manitou's hands.

I rose at sunrise. After a few bites of dried berries and
smoked fish I tried to sit quietly. I could not. The signifi‐
cance of the moment awaiting me stirred my restlessness,
so I went for a long easy swim instead.

It was only then, while I moved effortlessly through
the water, that I understood the source of my nervous‐
ness. I hadn't seen Kate during the night as I had hoped
to. I had kept one ear open for her all night and even
burned a hot, bright fire to attract her. Still she had not
come. This disappointed me. I was not aware that the
Kate had spent the night at the White Pine Inn preparing
for today's unique business opportunity.

So as I swam and felt the stiffness of the night disap‐
pear, I convinced myself that it was probably best that
she had not appeared. I did not know what I would have
said to her had she come. I only knew that I would not be
as nervous if she had.

After my morning swim I returned to the south vil‐
lage. I went to my *wigwom* and got my medicine bag. The

small sack held a Petoskey stone, the feather of an eagle, the claw of a muskrat and a few sacred herbs. An additional eagle feather and muskrat claw adorned the exterior of the deerskin satchel, as well as a beaded symbol of the Black Panther. Then I wrapped a woven blanket around my broad shoulders and solemnly walked to the only vehicle in the south village, a 1922 Ford Model T. Maymegwan and Sawmay met me there.

My people had decorated the automobile for today's festivities with an assortment of brightly colored ribbons and a variety of fetishes. Sawmay sat in the front seat next to May, who took the wheel. I climbed into the back and stood. I remained standing while the vehicle traveled slowly through the village. All along the way the people of Tawkenin greeted me with shouts of encouragement and handed me gifts and offerings. Some were devoutly reciting prayers. The back of the colorful Ford was overflowing when I finally took a seat. May accelerated the ancient vehicle and we headed to Bay View. In an hour, we were there.

Our unique chariot drew immediate attention and a crowd quickly gathered around the gaudy sedan. Sawmay and Maymegwan rose to face the crowd. Both had been reverently mute during the drive over. As I exited the car, Sawmay broke his silence.

"Remember that Tawkenin is our home, Aupetchi," he said emphatically, "where your spirit and the spirits of our ancestors live always. Today you must swim swiftly so our home can remain undisturbed."

I nodded solemnly in agreement. The truth of Sawmay's assertion refocused my concentration. I went to the marshalling area and registered for the race. My restlessness dissipated completely.

I silently repeated Sawmay's declaration over and over again. I repeated it while I removed the blanket and handed it to Maymegwan. She had finally escaped the curious throng that still surrounded the stoic Sawmay and our propitious vehicle.

"Good luck brother," she said as I handed her my medicine bag.

"Thank you," I replied.

I believed it would go well if I continued to reiterate Sawmay's charge, which I did faithfully. It filled my mind as I prepared for the start. "Tawkenin is our home, "where my spirit and the spirits of my ancestors live always. I must swim swiftly."

I knew this swim could secure the future for the Anabe and that all my previous swims had been to recapture our past. Today I had to be both fast and smart. The cleverest man would win, because he would need to selectively generate speed throughout the race. I knew Cole could beat me in a short sprint. I suspected Cole couldn't sustain his speed over such a long distance. I also understood that I did not have to actually win the race, I just had to beat Cole. Consequently I visualized a long, easy, effortless swim, just as I had done around the islands of Waugoshance. This knowledge softened the effect of my horrendous start.

Cole had been well prepared. He and one other swimmer surged ahead of everyone. I thought that such haste was foolish since the race could not be won at the start. As soon as I found myself trapped with the masses, I reconsidered. I understood why they ran so fast.

◆◆◆

Now I swam easily, although I was still concerned about being in the midst of the pack. This concern passed quickly as I worked it to my advantage. It helped me focus my concentration and I swiftly established my deep-water rhythm. I passed the rest of the field steadily and was in third by the time I passed the one-mile mark.

We were swimming in over forty feet of water. The blue, cloudless sky above us cloaked the tumultuous activity of Michi Gama, which undulated just beyond the shelter of Little Traverse Bay. Fueled by a strong northwest wind the water surged into the Bay from the giant lake. We were

pushed violently by breaking whitecaps. They altered our
course mercilessly. I learned later that fifty-four swimmers
dropped out of the race before they reached the two-mile
buoy. Escort boats ferried them ashore as quickly as they
could. Only the brave continued on.

This was my element. I surged forward, riding the
swells as if I were Odawgen during Memegot, swimming
between the south and the north village. Each descent refreshed me as I rode the waves forward and each ascent
taxed me as I maintained my beat. I felt positive about
my chances, even though I could not see Cole ahead of me.

I knew that Cole swam in swimming pools most of the
time. May had explained to me that when Cole swam in a
pool, he turned every twenty yards. Each turn provided
him with a slight breather, a chance to mildly recharge.
Here, in the deep open water, he had to swim constantly.
This was not his element. I also knew he would swim the
Australian crawl, the traditional competitive freestyle,
which would make breathing difficult. He normally
breathed to his left, but to do so in this water was to inhale Lake Michigan instead of air. Instead he would have
to exaggerate his right arm recovery, which would raise
his head so he could inhale air, which would disrupt his
rhythm. Consequently I knew that Cole would be struggling with the swells. I also knew that during his descent
his horizontal plane would streamline him beneath the
next ascending swell, forcing him to fight his way out.

Unfortunately for me, Cole's sister Olivia had anticipated our circumstance. She had trained Cole using both
a six-beat and four-beat kick, for stormy and mild
weather. Cole adopted the slower kick as he passed the
one-mile marker, and unbeknownst to me was moving up
on another *waubesh*, Jay Pond.

I learned later that Pond's life saving training served him
well. His stroke was unique, yet similar to my exaggerated head-out style. He lacked only my innate sense of
meter: Pond's cadence, dictated by the beat of his kick,

was faster. He kicked six beats per stroke to my three, which ironically worked against him. My unorthodox beat turned out to be most effective. My deep kick acted as a propeller on my descent, then as a stabilizing rudder on my ascent. Pond's kick was shallower; his propulsion came from his upper body only.

I finally saw the wake of the lead swimmers when I was a mile and a half into the race. The fact that there were two concerned me, but only mildly. I knew that one was Cole, and he was the man I needed to beat. By the two-mile buoy I had reduced the lead even more. Cole and Jay swam shoulder to shoulder ahead of me, with just under a mile to go, and I was gaining with every stroke. The tip of Harbor Point was now less than three hundred yards away and the lake was rapidly getting shallower.

As we passed over a rocky shoal ten feet below the surface Cole began to speed up. I learned later that he and Olivia had scouted this spot earlier in the week. It served as a marker for him, and when he passed above it he would establish his own pace regardless of what Jay or I did, or did not do.

Cole began by increasing the cadence of his kick. The lake became calm as we passed the point so he returned to his six-beat kick. He held his head low in the water so that the waterline passed at his hairline. The water depth now equaled that of the White Pine pool he knew so well, about five feet. Finally Cole was in his element.

Jay, despite his purposeful slow down, could not stay with Cole when he picked up the pace. Pond's strategy would have worked if Cole had faded; Jay had enough energy left to win. However Cole was not fading. Quite the contrary, he was picking up speed. Cole was swimming a smart tactical race, the one contingency Jay had not considered at this distance. For Jay Pond, the race was now effectively over as he imperceptibly fell further behind Cole on each and every stroke. He did not have a big enough lead, and Cole had too much left.

As we rounded the final buoy marking one half of a mile left to swim, Jay had fallen two body-lengths behind Cole and was less than a half a body-length ahead of me. As I breathed I noticed a band of Anabe standing on the tip of the Point, beneath the lighthouse. They cheered me as I swam by. Sawmay had joined the crowd and his cheers were the loudest of all.

I had spent most of the race not only behind the leaders, but wide of them as well. Only after I rounded the Point did I move closer to the pair. My sudden appearance startled Jay, who did not know I was so close. Abruptly he found himself looking not at a silver medal, but at a bronze. Moments ago he could see only gold. He tried to dig deep and fend off my charge, but fatigue overwhelmed Jay's body and it did not respond to his mind's weakening will.

I moved ahead of Jay and upon Cole's heels as the Anabe continued to whoop joyfully. They shouted encouragement as I swam past them towards the Harrison cottage.

As I moved next to Cole I hoped he would think I was Jay Pond returning. I think he did since he increased his pace, pulling and kicking stronger and deeper. Still, his lead diminished as we passed in front of the crowded Harrison dock. I knew that Cole couldn't believe that Jay Pond could sprint this quickly, this late in the race.

Cole did not know that it was I, Aupetchi, until he tried to catch a glimpse of his family while breathing. Olivia was crouching in the forefront of the screaming crowd. She extended both arms outward, towards him, with a gap of about ten inches between each hand. This represented the lead he now held. As he looked at Olivia he finally saw me. I could see the recognition register on his face. As I breathed towards shore I saw a man I knew to be Cole's father. His posture communicated displeasure. His head was buried in his hands and his back faced the finish line.

The lead changed hands often as we furiously swam the final eighty yards. First I surged ahead, only to have my move countered by Cole. With fifty yards to go I moved ahead again, followed by Cole who retook the lead on the very next stroke. He held it for three strokes before my deep kick accelerated me back into first.

The Anabe followed along as we swam near the shore. They intermingled with the Harrison clan and their cronies as the crowd moved onto the dock that served as the finish line. Kate had abandoned her post with Helen at the sound of the first Anabe whoop and now joined the multitude fighting for a clear view of the finish. The pier sagged under the weight of the wild mob gathered to witness the exciting end.

With twenty yards to go Cole took his last breath and stroked furiously towards the finish, again moving slightly ahead of me. He held the lead for fifteen yards before my kick ignited me one final time and accelerated me forcefully towards the wall. Instinctively I rolled my body and fully extended my right arm, finishing with my fingers stretched. As I touched the dock I looked through the lake water and watched for Cole's touch, which I saw clearly.

Cole reached furiously for the wall, trying to out touch me. He turned to his left in time to see my fingertips strike the submerged portion of the dock. An instant later Cole finished by grabbing the dock's top edge. Then he dropped his head into the water in defeat. He did not streamline his finish and because of that he had lost.

My momentum was so strong that I ricocheted off the wall after I touched. As I drifted backwards I permitted myself a small smile, knowing that I had done all I could and that it had been enough. I had won. Manitou had been kind to me, and to my people. Regaining my composure I looked up stoically and saw Kate working her way through the crowd. Cole did not see her; instead he wrapped an arm around me and whispered into my ear, too tired to speak at full volume.

"I don't know how you did it, but you got me," he said.

Kate arrived dockside and kneeled down next to the two of us. My eyes met hers and much to my surprise she shrugged inconclusively. Then she reached down next to me and caressed Cole's head, which he held in folded arms while resting on the dock.

"Good swim Cole," she said, "it looks like you won."

Her comment stunned me. Cole reacted to Kate's claim with an inquisitive look. Neither of us realized that to Kate and most of the crowd, Cole's high finish above the water line was far more noticeable than my underwater touch. Not only was his finish clearly visible to all, but a small splash preceded it that gave the illusion that he had touched milliseconds earlier than he actually had. Consequently, it appeared to most as though Cole had finished the race before me.

Seconds later, Jay Pond finished. He looked around him and noticed that neither Cole nor I seemed joyful. We were both hanging onto the lip of dock and looking questionably towards the trio of judges huddled above us.

"Good race," he said to each of us between breaths. "So who won anyway?"

I looked to Cole to tell him, as he had just told me. But things had changed, quickly and dramatically. This was now the question everyone wanted answered. Cole had admitted to me that I had beaten him. I knew this too; to us it was obvious. But now Kate's statement had silenced him. Cole realized, well before me, that the race judges would determine the official final results. It was that close a finish. He had been in this situation before.

Cole knew that in this time, before the development of touch pads and state-of-the-art timing systems, judges' decisions often decided close races. In fact, Cole's high school win streak had been extended because of it. His team had traveled to swim the Hawken School. Although

Western Reserve had won easily, Cole faced Hawken's best swimmer, Larry Baker. Cole's teammate, Jim "Buffalo" Beardsley, also chose this day to swim the race of his life.

The 60-yard Freestyle had ended in a dead heat. The "official" times, affected as they were back then by human error, had Baker winning with a time of 28.0. They clocked Beardsley at 28.2 and Cole at 28.4. Despite this data the judges unanimously and accurately named Cole the winner, Baker second and Beardsley third. This was because the timers had timed inaccurately, while the judge's saw the order of finish clearly.

I knew nothing of such doings. To me the race was over and the results were clear. I had won, and Cole Harrison must honor his promise. I had saved Tawkenin.

Meanwhile, race officials huddled together and checked the times recorded on the stopwatches assigned for each of the competitors. Two-dozen stopwatches had been started when the gun fired at Bay View. Then a race official drove them around the bay to the finish line. The watches timed the top two finishers in each of twelve categories. The official timers stopped them by hand when their swimmer finished, or when they thought their swimmer had finished.

The unruly crowd that overtook the pier had complicated this apparently simple task. The timers, as well as the officials, had to jockey for position. Each ended up with an obstructed view; none were standing directly above the swimmers, as they should have been. Had they been, they would have seen the actual finish and they would have secured an accurate time. They would have seen me win, as they would have looked down into the water and seen my hand. Instead, most saw Cole's splash from the side, while few could accurately guess when I had actually touched.

Despite the challenge the timers performed very well. The timer assigned to Cole had a clocking of 1:23:08.7

seconds. My timer clocked me at 1:23:08.2, a half a second ahead. However, the three judges reached a split decision. The two who stood furthest from the edge of the dock thought Cole had won. The third, who had retained his position well, knew that I had won. The discussion became heated.

As the judges mulled over their decision, Cole, Jay and I gathered together away from the crowd. Cole placed one arm around my shoulder, the other around Jay's.

"You really got me," he finally said, in full voice. "Not by much, but you got me. That was a whale of a finish."

"Congratulations chief," Jay chimed in, nodding towards Cole. "I don't know where you learned to swim like that but I'm glad someone beat this bum."

"And how," teased Cole. "The important thing is that we both beat Pond scum, so this is a truly glorious day."

"I am victorious," I said with pride. "Tawkenin will stay with the Anabe."

"Only if the judges agree," Cole replied. "They have the final say of course, but it looked pretty obvious to me."

I ignored the good-natured ribbing between the two veterans and mulled over Cole's last comment. What could be more final than the consensus of the combatants? Confused, I left the two *waubesh* swimmers and approached my people. They were waiting for me quietly, respectfully. Sawmay stopped me in front of the swarm.

"Did you beat him?" he inquired.

"I did, and he knows it," I replied truthfully.

The Anabe were overjoyed with the news and cheered deliriously. Troubled by their outburst I raised my hand to silence my people.

"Be still," I ordered. The crowd became quiet. "We can't be sure of this yet."

"Can't be sure of what?" Maymegwan asked as she emerged from the crowd. "That you won?"

"Not that I won, Cole has admitted that. But they will decide who will be named the winner, which may not be me," I answered.

"The *waubesh* judges?" Sawmay questioned. "Deciding between a *waubash* and an Anabe? That cannot be."

But Sawmay had witnessed the animated discussion among the officials and quickly understood. As I left the Anabe to report to the awards ceremony, Sawmay explained the situation to the people. The three men in starched white shirts would determine the winner of the race. As the Anabe absorbed this fact, Sawmay, spat savagely in the direction of the distant officials. The Anabe understood immediately. Cole was *waubesh*, the officials were *waubesh* and the race was a *waubesh* event. A *waubesh* would certainly win.

I joined Jay and Cole, who stood with Kate, and stoically awaited the final announcement. An awards stand had been erected allowing the top three finishers in each category to be seen by the crowd. Cole quietly confided to Jay.

"I can't believe that Indian beat us. He's another Jim Thorpe," he said.

"No kidding," Pond agreed. "Do you think he'll get the judges decision?"

"Who knows. I hope not, I have to much riding on this," Cole answered.

Kate overheard bits and pieces of the conversation and came to join us. As she passed behind me she gently placed her hand on my back while moving towards Cole.

"What's up sweetie?" she asked. "Is there going to be a judges decision?"

"There'd better be," Cole answered.

"Ladies and gentlemen," the announcer interrupted, "we have the final results of the Open Division." The crowd grew quiet. "In third place, with a time of 1:23:12.7 seconds: Jay Pond from Glen Haven."

The crowd cheered as Jay took the stand and accepted the bronze medal.

"In second place, as a result of a judges' decision..."

Cole jumped to his feet and hugged Kate tightly before the announcer could continue.

"...with a time of 1:23.08.2, proudly representing our Anabe neighbors, Aupetchi."

Stunned and disbelieving I hypnotically climbed the awards stand and numbly accepted the silver medal. A few tears escaped from me, which I discreetly wiped away. I looked down at Kate, whom Cole had abandoned for the well-wishers surrounding him, and noticed that she too was crying. She did not wipe her tears away.

Cole bounced up the awards stand as they declared him the winner. He held his gold medal high above his head. The locals cheered while movement in the back of the crowd marked the departure of the Anabe faithful. They surrounded and consoled me, and escorted me to the beach.

Four joined Cole on the stand and commandeered the announcer's microphone.

"People of Harbor Springs," he declared as he squeezed Cole's jaw, "recognize this face, and remember this name. Cole Harrison will continue to make Emmet County proud."

The crowd cheered again and began to chant. "Helsinki, Harrison! Helsinki, Harrison!"

Cole's Olympic die was cast, at my expense.

Chapter Eleven

FULL MOON

Friday, September 8

COLE

After I won the gold medal my father turned my life into chaos. It started when Four called Coach Wilson after the race and urged him to seize this opportunity. I was woken with a five a.m. phone call from Coach Wilson the next morning. He spoke to me at length about his training plans for my Olympic quest. I knew then that my father had called, as Coach Wilson and I had never discussed the Olympics.

Furthermore, Four filled all my afternoons after the win with meetings. I met with all the principles involved in the real estate development plan. The first task we accomplished was to agree upon the name of the development: Gold Medal Village. Then, on the Tuesday after Labor Day, the town clerk issued a clearance for our group to develop the land. The day after that the Anabe were informed that they must move.

The intensity of Four's sudden involvement in my life overwhelmed me. I had seen the disappointment in his face when I swam past the family cottage, engaged in the race of my life. That chagrin had vanished with my victory, and was replaced by an immense pride. He boasted to all that would listen that I could beat anyone in the state and that I would win an Olympic Gold Medal. He now catered to my every wish.

I still thought I had a good shot at qualifying for the Helsinki games. Unlike my father, however, I felt less sure about winning a medal, any medal. I knew that no matter how much I prepared, the Olympics were a crapshoot. Nevertheless, the win improved my confidence for two reasons. First, I was swimming better than ever. I had finally mastered both speed and endurance. Second, one man whom I knew could beat me – Aupetchi · would not swim in the Olympics. Aupetchi had swum his one and only race.

So for the first time I could remember my father and I

enjoyed each other's company. Every day had been a good day since the race, which was fortunate since the exhilaration I felt each day was balanced by the turmoil I experienced each evening.

Much to my surprise Kate had grown more distant since the race. My dream of matrimony now seemed improbable. The only solace I had was that she still hadn't said "no." Now she simply refused to discuss the proposal. She was obsessed with the outcome of the race. Her early congratulations had turned sour, all because I had admitted to her that I thought Aupetchi had touched first. She didn't understand how I could consider myself the winner.

I tried to explain that the judges determined the official order of finish in every race. The official times usually supported their decision, but when they did not the judges' decision was always final. The human eye was more accurate than a hand held clock. Every swimmer understood this. I told her that it was like an umpire calling balls and strikes in baseball. It didn't matter if the pitcher, the catcher, the batter and everyone else in the ballpark thought a pitch was a strike; if the umpire called it a ball, it was a ball. It was the same in competitive swimming. If the judges declared you the winner, you won. The judges had declared me the winner, so I won. It was that simple. And because I got the gold medal, and Aupetchi did not, I did not feel obligated to recognize the Anabe claim to Tawkenin. That land should rightly become Gold Medal Village.

Kate disagreed, even though she conceded that I was the official winner. She questioned whether or not I was honoring the intent of my wager with Aupetchi, the wager she had brokered. She believed that the judges' opinions were irrelevant. The declared winner of the race wasn't necessarily the winner of the bet. She insisted that the bet was simply who would swim fastest and finish first, not who the judges declared to be the winner. It was a fine yet significant point.

More so after I admitted that Aupetchi finished first, and especially after Maymegwan told Kate that Aupetchi knew this as well. Kate knew that both contestants agreed that I did touch second. To her credit, Kate didn't insist that I surrender my gold medal or relinquish the honor that went with the title. She simply wanted me to do the honorable thing, as she put it. To her this meant being honest, with Aupetchi and with myself. This meant waiving my claim to the title of Tawkenin.

"Search your heart for the answer, Cole. Search your heart. If it honestly tells you not to admit that Aupetchi won the wager, then build your stupid houses," she had said, before adding with sarcasm, "It's not like they need the land."

I hadn't responded.

"But if you do build them, Cole, you should know that I will never live on that stolen land," she added.

And so it went. Every time we got together after the race we each hoped the other would revise their position, only to learn that the other was steadfast. Finally, in a last gasp effort, I suggested that we should take a trip on my family's cruiser, the *Lumber Baron*. I hoped we would benefit by leaving Harbor Springs for a day or two so I suggested that we go on an overnight. Kate reluctantly agreed, despite the social taboo placed upon such behavior.

We left early in the morning, six days after the race and one hour after sunrise. I did not retain the services of our boatman since I wanted to be alone with Kate. I elected to serve as captain, helmsman and navigator on the 35-foot craft. Kate would crew.

The trip south started smoothly. We traveled easily on the calm lake, crossing the mouth of Grand Traverse Bay without incident before refueling in Northport. Then we enjoyed a leisurely lunch in Leland's bustling Fishtown before returning to the lake in the late afternoon. The sky was blue, as it had been all day, and the lake was still quiet.

We were satiated and content as the *Lumber Baron* motored into Sleeping Bear Bay. I followed the Manitou Passage, heading to Frankfort where we would spend the night. By all accounts the day had been a success. I slowed the *Lumber Baron* and passed to the lee of North Manitou Island. The massive Sleeping Bear Dune loomed protectively off our port. Numerous pleasure craft and an ore freighter sailed the Bay with us.

The calm water relaxed us. We were comfortable in each other's presence, despite the discord. We did genuinely like each other and we tolerated the other's quiet introspection well. The only chill between us was a sporadic blast of brisk Canadian air, not the philosophical chasm.

After passing North Manitou I turned northwest to travel through the channel that separated the islands. I moved towards the open lake, leaving the lee of South Manitou behind me.

Kate and I huddled together in the *Lumber Baron's* raised pilothouse, finding snug shelter from the cool early-autumn air. Then Kate wrapped a wool blanket around her and stretched out on a soft leather-covered bench.

Fifteen minutes later Kate was asleep, her head resting on a Mackinaw jacket that had been left onboard. A low cloud cover had moved in quickly, cloaking the northern third of Lake Michigan. I could see scattered lighting bolts on the horizon, less than twenty miles away. Suddenly I felt isolated. I wished that I had noticed earlier that we were alone on the open lake. All ship traffic had been in the Manitou Passage, no doubt seeking safe harbor from the lake's volatile wrath.

"No matter how bad it gets in the passage, it's fifty times worse on the lake," veteran sailors always said.

The leeward passage was always the best choice when the weather turned. And it was clear to me that the weather had turned. I quickly regretted my decision to explore the northwest shore of South Manitou, the windward shore.

I had come this way because I hoped to find a secluded harbor where Kate and I could anchor and revisit our impasse. I wanted to tell her again that I knew Aupetchi touched first. I wanted to tell her that I knew in my heart that Aupetchi had won.

Not that this meant I was going to waive my claim to Tawkenin. I was not eager to interrupt the flow of admiration coming from my father. I had waited my whole life for that. Certainly the kind-hearted Kate could appreciate this. Instead I had planned on announcing a compromise I had devised. I had even obtained Four's reluctant approval before we had disembarked.

To appease Kate I would offer the Anabe the first right of purchase to select home sites, individually or collectively, at a reduced price. Even if the entire Anabe population opted to take advantage of this option, they would inhabit less than five percent of the available acreage. I could then develop what was left. That way Kate and I could still live in our dream house, and we would be very rich. And best of all, my father approved.

I had high hopes for this compromise, especially since I would give Maymegwan and Aupetchi prime home sites free of charge. I believed this would clinch the deal.

Suddenly a howl of cold wind roared through the open windows of the pilothouse and redirected my attention to our tenuous situation, which had worsened. Within five minutes we would face squalls topping 30 knots, forcing me to alter my course. The west-northwest winds made my intended tack impossible to follow. I feared that the *Lumber Baron* would founder so I turned her into the wind. The erupting horizon moved closer. I could not ride this storm out; I needed to find safe harbor, now.

I altered my course slightly, powering further out into the menacing lake. The ship tossed with a lurch as a strong gust hit her broadside as we topped a swell. Despite the danger I held against the wind so I could reposition the *Lumber Baron* and reverse course east-southeast, putting the powerful gusts behind us. Then I could ride the incoming waves and slip between the two islands to safe harbor in Sleeping Bear Bay.

Kate woke suddenly as the mahogany craft pitched and creaked under the strain of the riotous elements beating upon it. She looked to the stern. The sight of the islands fading behind us alarmed her. She looked to the bow and the sight of the open lake churning violently openly frightened her.

"Cole, what are you doing? Turn around and get into the passage now!" she screamed.

"A few more minutes hon," I yelled loud enough to be heard over the storm.

"Hurry Cole, we shouldn't be in the open water," she howled as she moved next to me.

I placed a protective arm around her shoulders and drew her close.

"I know Kate, we'll turn back soon. Don't worry. We'll be all right," I shouted.

KATE

I wasn't so sure. The nightmare of my father's death haunted me as the *Lumber Baron* struggled against the surf. My father had actually been in my dream just moments ago: I had been walking with him on our beach, as a child. He held my small hand in his and talked lovingly to me, his only daughter. We looked ahead of us and saw Aupetchi standing in waist-high in the water. My father's spirit and presence had calmed my sleep; however even in my dream I could not understand why Aupetchi was standing in the water.

I was rudely wakened when the boat lurched forward, knocking my head into a paneled wall. I thought another boat had hit us. My vision became blurred. I collected myself, willing my focus to return. Just as it did the boat convulsed again. I wrapped my arms around Cole's waist and hugged him tightly, finding both support and security.

I noticed and admired Cole's intense concentration. Truth be told it surprised me. His single-minded sense of purpose convinced me that he possessed the skills needed to guide the *Lumber Baron* to safe harbor. I felt relatively hopeful, albeit anxious and bruised. The heart of the storm was still distant and the protective lee was just under five minutes away, if we turned in now.

My thoughts seem to guide Cole's action as he turned the *Lumber Baron* abeam with the wind. The floundering vessel's violent pitch turned into a dizzying roll. Cole held the wheel and maintained his position. Over two hundred horses strained beneath us as the motor rumbled to hold the course, to follow Cole's will. After what seemed an eternity the roll waned and the pitch returned as the *Lumber Baron* completed her turn. The bow plunged into the surging water and a violent mist blinded the view.

Suddenly my dread intensified. Images of my father filled my head once again. I knew that he had faced similar circumstances many years earlier and responded, as far as I knew, heroically. Cole was doing the same. But I knew the price of my father's bravery was death. I now wondered if Cole and I would share his fate. This thought changed my calm to terror. Suddenly I became hysterical and grabbed Cole by his collar, clinging to him as he struggled to pilot the floundering vessel.

"We're going die out here, damn it," I yelled accusingly.

The surf crashed around us, filling the cabin with spray and flushing three portable captains' chairs overboard. I clenched my fists and screamed. Another wave rushed through the cabin, knocking both of us to the deck.

"God help us!" I pleaded, struggling to stand again. I pulled on the helm to lift myself. Cole was dazed and took a few moments longer to get back on his feet. When he did he grabbed the wheel from my hands and fought to regain control. But it was too late. I had pulled the *Lumber Baron* off course. As a result we overshot the passage entrance between the two islands.

"Calm down, Kate," he ordered, shouting to be heard above the roar that enveloped us. "You have to calm down. If we loose our cool we'll drown, if we stay calm we might survive. So shut up and calm down. Now!"

I stopped screaming. I knew Cole's order should be followed. Hysteria would not help. I struggled to regain control of my emotions. I tried to make sense of the situation. Perhaps it was my destiny to survive because my father had not? I decided to embrace his spirit and fight to survive.

"Calm it is, Cole," I said reassuringly.

Cole paused to consider my sudden repose. My eyes were steady and my hands still. My panic had vanished, but our peril endured.

"Secure the window latches, get the life jackets, and then close the pilothouse door," he directed.

I followed his command. I put on my life jacket,

handed him his, secured the latches, and locked the door. This reduced the mist inside the cabin and quieted the roar surrounding us. Meanwhile the boat found a rhythm. The peril seemed to dissipate. As we re-approached the channel we saw the benevolent glow of a bonfire. It was ablaze on the beach of the small peninsula that we needed to pass to find shelter. I sensed the worst was over. I would not die as my father had.

Then, without warning, a fourteen-foot wave broke high above us. We were sitting in a six-foot trough created by the preceding wave and were riding too low in the water. The rogue wave crashed into the *Lumber Baron*. She rolled to her starboard as her bow pitched forward. The whitecap shattered the protective glass of the pilothouse and the elements violently invaded our safe haven.

A second ghoulish whitecap immediately followed and capsized our small vessel. The doorframe collapsed, making it impossible to open. When we went under the surface the space quickly flooded, making it eerily quiet. I was trapped in the overturned pilothouse. My tightly secured life jacket made it impossible for me to escape. I bobbed like a cork against the deck that was now above me. I could not open the damaged door, and the bulk of the jacket made me too big to squeeze through a broken window. I became disoriented and distressed.

I had lost Cole. I saw him climbing through a broken window in the pilothouse just as the second wave had hit. Unlike me, I think he saw it coming. Unlike me, he did not have his life jacket on. Then, as if I willed him to appear, he came to me.

He struggled through the sandy flotsam into the flooded, capsized cabin, pulling himself back through a window that was edged with jagged glass. He found me struggling in a blind panic to save myself. Cole kept his distance while reaching for my wrist. He grabbed it firmly then pivoted me in the water so I could not instinctively lunge at him, thereby preventing me from holding him under against his will. With my back to him he reached around me, un-strapped my life jacket and stripped it from me.

Then he pushed me through a window and to the surface. I gasped for air when I broke through, and turned to Cole, but he wasn't there. He hadn't followed me; he hadn't broken the surface. I coughed up water from my lungs and desperately embraced the capsized hull, searching for any sign of Cole.

I did not know it but Cole had gotten stuck underwater while saving me. He frantically tried to free himself, but the lack of air rendered his effort futile. He quickly collapsed from exhaustion and fell unconscious. His limp body began to drift aimlessly, anchored only by his right foot, which was wedged in the shattered glass of a broken window.

Above him I worked to catch my breath while considering my options. I knew that Cole had to be struggling beneath me, near me. I had to go find him despite the risk. I took three quick breaths and was just about to go after him when I heard someone shout.

"Stop!" the voice commanded.

I scanned the surf around me, trying to find the source.

AUPETCHI

In the week following the race my people begrudgingly accepted the results. We had to; there was no apparent recourse. The Anabe knew that I had beaten the *waubesh* swimmer. It was difficult to accept that the official outcome was final, that we could not alter the *waubesh* judge's decision. But we did. Cole Harrison had won and now wore the gold medal. I had to settle for the silver, no matter how tarnished it was in our eyes. The injustice was reality.

This became clear four days after the race, when a battalion of bulldozers, tractors, backhoes and land movers appeared on the southern border of Tawkenin. They sat there still, patiently waiting for the final *waubesh* government approvals. Then they would ambush and destroy our homeland.

Despite these troubling circumstances we continued with our daily tasks. One of the most important of these was our annual fishing trip to the waters surrounding Mishe Mokwa. I had joined the group young and was now a veteran; this was my tenth trip. Only four of the twenty-man band had more experience. I knew my role and fulfilled my obligations well, despite the fact that I was restless. I could not get the race out of my mind. I had let my people down.

Sawmay had tried to reassure me after that dreadful race. As we had left the pier together, following the disappointed Anabe who had come to cheer me on, the wise man made a terse pronouncement.

"Manitou's will was done," he had said.

I could not accept this. How could it be so, I wondered? My disbelief intensified when the construction equipment arrived. Tawkenin teetered on the precipice of extinction, which could not be Manitou's wish. To lose our homeland in such a way was his will? This bitter twist of fate was the best the Anabe could expect after following

Manitou so faithfully? The sage's acceptance of this circumstance disturbed me and provided me with no
comfort.

Worse yet I knew I had beaten Cole, we both know it.
Cole had told me so, twice. I despised my silver medal. It
represented the ultimate betrayal, by Cole, by the
waubesh and by Manitou.

◆◆◆

Now, days later, I found it hard to concentrate on
fishing. I was unusually oblivious of the environment surrounding me and the sudden storm that quickly
enveloped the waters made sacred by Mishe Mokwa
caught me by surprise. The fish had been nervous long
before the clouds appeared on the horizon, so today's catch
had been small. The storm forced us to return to our island camp, where we sheltered ourselves in temporary
spruce-covered *wigwoms*. The gale whipped through the
treetops above us. Branches snapped explosively around
us. We huddled in our shelters and warmed ourselves in
front of our fires. Everyone, that is, except me.

I had noticed the silhouette of a small craft moving
into the open lake earlier in the day, just before I became
lost in my disillusionment. I remembered this because I
thought then that the sailor was foolhardy. I wondered if
Mishe Mokwa would watch over the boat while she maintained her silent vigil, waiting for her two cubs.

Now I knew it be would suicidal if the craft remained
on the open lake. This storm was too violent, even for the
sacred mother bear. So I banked the fire in my small *wigwom* and left the security of the camp. I went to tend to
the bonfire we had built — used to mark our camp while
fishing. I thought it could be a valuable beacon to this er-
rant craft. I had to do something.

The wind calmed and the roar of the wake mellowed
as I moved through the woods that protected our camp. I
approached the fire that still burned on the small sandy
peninsula. The eye of the storm was above me so I worked

quickly. I knew that this brief calm disguised a hidden fe-
rocity waiting to strike again. I pulled large pine logs from
a shelter and added them to the tenacious fire. The timber
roared as it ignited into flame, illuminating the lakeshore
surrounding me. Then, through the eerie calm, I heard an
unfamiliar noise that startled me. I knew that storms
could create some strange howls, but what I heard was
human: a human scream.

I looked furtively out into the gloomy surf, trying to
locate the source of the wail. I scanned the horizon and
saw nothing. I looked again and again until I finally per-
ceived a slight movement with my peripheral vision. I
looked to my left, inspecting the waterline anxiously. An
obliging flash of approaching lighting profiled the small
craft struggling against the lake. It was less than fifty
yards from the rocky shore. I knew the craft was too small
to survive the impact if it floundered here. The shore
would destroy the boat.

I instinctively rushed into the raging water, taking no
time for my usual ritual. I had to act immediately. I
struggled through the incoming waves, slipping often on
the slick rock bottom, bruising myself in the process. I
crawled through the forceful surf, finally moving far
enough from shore that the bottom became sand. I began
to move more quickly. I crouched on the lake bottom as
swells passed over me, and then thrust myself out, and
forward, through the trough that followed.

I could see that they were too close to shore. The
power of the surf exceeded the strength of the ship's engine. I understood completely that they were at the mercy
of the lake. Finally I saw someone clinging to the overturned hold. I thought I was imagining things when I
realized it was Kate.

"Stop!" I yelled to her.

Adrenaline, and the spirit of Mishe Mokwa, filled my
veins as I dove beneath the surface and swam towards
her, underwater. The relative calm enabled me to move

swiftly. I resurfaced twice for air before I reached her. I
tried to grab her and guide her to shore.

"Leave me alone!" she argued while resisting my efforts. "Cole is still down there, I've got to go get him."

"No," I insisted, "I will go. You stay here or you too
may perish."

It was then that she looked in my eyes, and I believe
recognized me. She nodded in agreement.

"Go, now," she said.

I hesitated, still worried about her safety. "If you drift
any closer to shore you have to leave the boat," I instructed.

"Get Cole damn it, go get Cole," she countered, "or I
will! He must still be in the pilot house."

"I will get him. Remember the submerged rocks close
to shore will kill you if you are with the boat when it
crashes into them," I reiterated before diving below the
tumultuous surface.

And then I decided to save the man who was stealing
my homeland. I wondered if Cole would do the same for
me. I suspected he would not.

I dove under. I could hold my breath for more than
two minutes in ordinary circumstances. The intense storm
and turbulent water demanded extraordinary exertion so
I figured I had a minute and a half, at best. I located Cole
quickly; he was trapped just below the surface. His last
image before losing consciousness must have been of Kate
gulping in the air just above him.

The murky water whipping around me created a frenzied crimson-tinted film. I traced Cole's torso and moved
down his leg until I located his snared appendage. I desperately grabbed at his disjointed foot and tried to pull it
free. Despite being unconscious, Cole's body instinctively
recoiled in pain.

Above us Kate flinched in horror at the image that
greeted her after following my shallow dive. She finally
saw Cole, just below the surface. His serene, lifeless face

was less than a foot from her. At that moment she knew exactly how much she loved him. She immediately tried to resuscitate him, inhaling deeply, dropping her head below the surface and exhaling into his unresponsive lungs. There was nothing else to do. She continued to do this as the shattered hull moved closer to shore with each slap of a wave.

Beneath her I moved closer to the mangled foot's hazy outline. More than 70 seconds had passed. I pulled the foot towards me, but it remained lodged. I needed to return to the surface soon, but I decided to try to free him one more time. I knew that the longer Cole was submerged, the less desirable it was to retrieve him. At some point, an honorable death would be preferable to a meaningless life. I had to give it one more go. With my last bit of energy I pulled the foot downward and away from the jagged frame. The water turned bright red. I had opened a laceration created by the shattered glass, but Cole's foot was free.

Kate felt Cole release and pulled his limp body towards her while I pushed him to the surface. Together we moved him precariously onto the hull. I ripped off my leggings and quickly bandaged Cole's spurting wounds as best I could. Now naked, I paused to catch my breath and recover from the ordeal. Kate continued to attend to Cole, filling his lungs with her breath and maintaining pressure on his wound, hoping to revive him.

"We must go, now," I commanded.

I pushed away from the hull and struggled to stand in the water. In a moment I stabilized myself, bouncing on my toes off the sand below me and leaning into the rushing water surrounding me. I came back towards the hull until I was two feet away from the dying Cole and his faithful Kate, still clinging to the thrashed skeleton of the *Lumber Baron*.

"Push him towards me," I shouted while motioning to

Kate. "The boat's going to crash any time now. We'll dress his wounds ashore. You will both die if you stay."

As if cued, the fragile craft moaned loudly. Kate prodded Cole off the hull and I snared him quickly. The sea swelled behind us. Kate leapt from the remains of the once proud *Lumber Baron* just as it's weary timber snapped. The tail section splintered, smashing the inverted mahogany rails. The underwater rocks and boulders that protected Michi Gama's shore would quickly claim another victim. A twelve-foot whitecap confirmed the destruction.

The surging waters propelled Kate forward, flotsam battering her as she struggled. She worked her way to shore, focusing now only on her survival. Meanwhile I tenaciously held my position, dodging the flotsam and cradling Cole's bruised body. I mimicked Kate's resuscitation efforts while awkwardly struggling to carry him to shore. After an eternity, I placed Cole on the sand, then collapsed next to him on the beach. A clap of thunder crashed directly above us.

Kate found us near the persistent fire. She ran to us and helped move Cole off the peninsula, into the protective forest. There, behind a stand of birch and below a canopy of pine, Cole twitched in her arms. His eyes snapped open alertly and he vomited a mixture of bile, lake water, and blood. He gasped for air. Cole was alive. We were all alive. We had survived. Mishe Mokwa had come to our aid.

Chapter Twelve

WANING QUARTER

Thursday, September 14

KATE

T he dramatic rescue metamorphosed my feelings for Cole. I loved him completely, unconditionally. He had nothing more to prove to me. I knew that Cole was a good man, that he had honor and that I would marry him.

Cole demonstrated his strength of character when he bravely guided the *Lumber Baron* through the sudden storm. He had heroically rescued me after the vessel floundered. To me, this action revealed his moral fiber and demonstrated the depth of his love for me. The shipwreck changed my outlook completely - our shipwreck, not my father's. Ours. My appreciation for life and my relationship with Cole both changed dramatically that day.

After the wreck I visited Cole every day in Emmet County Memorial Hospital, helping him recover from his injury. I held his hand, read to him, and told him time and again that I would marry him, anytime and anyplace. And that was before he told me about the plan he had wanted to surprise me with on our fateful journey. He explained how the Anabe could live on Tawkenin forever, at least on a portion of it. He shared his desire to house Maymegwan and Aupetchi for free. Although it wasn't an ideal solution, I understood that it was a reasonable compromise. Cole had stood up to Four by persuading him to support these terms. This was a benchmark moment for Cole.

I appreciated Cole's offer, yet knew that it might not be enough to appease the Anabe. My last meeting with Maymegwan had convinced me of this. May had told me then that if the Anabe were forced to leave Tawkenin it would destroy the social and cultural adhesive that held her people together.

I knew that Cole's compromise would unquestionably alter the lives of the Anabe. I also knew it was probably the best possible solution. It was now the only option that would enable the Anabe to stay on their land, albeit a small parcel of it. I also knew the Anabe well enough to be sure that they could adapt if they stayed; the quality of their character was strong.

I no longer blamed Cole for the injustice. He had done all that he could, more than most *waubesh* in his position would have done. Certainly, he'd done more than I had expected he would. Civilization was attacking Tawkenin, not Cole Harrison. He was just a player in a game he did not invent, a game in which the rules were always changing.

Earlier this morning Cole's doctor had announced that he would release Cole from the hospital this afternoon. The news had prompted Cole to reach for my hand.

"Kate, do me a favor."

"Anything Cole, anything," I had replied.

"Go get Aupetchi for me. Tell him I want to meet him at your beach, at Bliss Beach. I want to see him today as soon as I get out. I want to see the man who has beaten me. Ask his sister, and Olivia to come too."

Although it was late afternoon when he was released, the sun was still high. I escorted Cole out of Emmet County Memorial Hospital. His foot was heavily bandaged, but he could walk with a cane. The doctor expected him to recover fully. We drove to my house where we parked the car. Then I helped him negotiate the trace that led to the shore. I told him we could bring Aupetchi, Maymegwan, and Olivia to him, but he was determined to get to the beach. When we finally arrived the two Anabe and Olivia rose to meet us. We all exchanged cordial, albeit strained greetings. Maymegwan spoke first.

"Kate, Cole, I hear congratulations are in order," she announced.

As May spoke Olivia presented five long stemmed crystal goblets and a bottle of champagne she had been hiding behind some dune grass. May filled the glasses, then spoke again.

"Cole, you must excuse me," she said, "but Kate told me of your plan to marry her. I am so happy for you both. And now I propose a toast. I hope the spirit of Manitou is with you, always and forever."

AUPETCHI

Olivia responded to May's toast with a cheer, and to avoid embarrassment I added some polite applause. May persuaded me to take an obligatory sip, which I did before moving away from the group. I could not pretend to be calm while I fumed inside. It had taken the collective persuasive powers of Maymegwan and the indefatigable Kate to convince me to even honor Cole's bizarre request to visit him. I saw no reason to travel to see a dishonorable man, much less celebrate with him.

Then Cole cleared his throat, interrupting my thoughts. He had moved quietly to my side.

"Au-pet-chi," he said respectfully, insuring phonetic accuracy, "that is how you say it, isn't it? Aupetchi."

"That is how it is said."

"Good. Thanks May," Cole continued, acknowledging my sister for coaching him on the pronunciation. "Aupetchi, I know you must wonder why I asked you to be here. I know you do not want to see me, that you feel I have done you wrong and hurt your people."

"What I know about you is that you do not keep your word," was all I said in reply.

Cole accepted my appraisal gracefully. He nodded his head knowingly then offered me his right hand, which I did not accept. Cole continued anyway.

"I asked you here for a reason," Cole explained. "Congratulations, champ. You win. I don't know how you did it but you did. You beat me, fair and square. You are the champion, Aupetchi, not me."

I looked into Cole's eyes for a long moment. The beach was unusually quiet, our companions completely attentive. I considered what words I could say in reply, squinted a bit, cocked my head, and then reached for Cole's still-extended hand. He gripped mine firmly and we shook.

"Yes, thank you," I said.

Cole continued to speak.

"I can't believe I'm saying this to someone who never raced before, but you are the better swimmer. Your skills are superior to mine. When we bet, we bet man-to-man, just you and I, on who would win. I understand that now. And you came to race, Aupetchi. I respect that most of all. Ours was the most satisfying race of my life. I gave everything I had, and still lost."

Cole gave Kate a wink and placed his free arm around her. My grip remained firm and my eyes stayed locked upon Cole's. He continued.

"You swam not just for yourself, or for your family: you swam for your nation. Our race was your Olympics. Now, because of you, I have a chance to win my Olympics. You have shown me how to be a champion. Most importantly though, you have helped me understand the meaning of dignity and honor."

I did not speak, but my face flushed with warmth and I felt my tense lips relax. I smiled. Maymegwan spoke for me.

"Thank you Cole."

"I know you really deserve the gold medal," Cole went on, "but the results are official. It wouldn't make a difference anyway, who gets the medal, that is. Besides, you deserve so much more than a gold medal, which is fake anyway. It's only silver you know, just like yours. It's just gold plating."

"I need no medals," I agreed.

"Exactly! And I do. So I'll keep it. What you need is this," Cole said while sweeping his arm, pointing along our coastal vista towards Tawkenin.

"I do not understand," I said with some impatience.

"Me neither," Kate agreed.

"Just tell her, little brother," spoke Olivia.

"This is your home," Cole said.

May smiled, as did Olivia. Only Kate and I did not know what Cole had planned.

"This is my home?" I repeated, then added caustically, "You mean this was my home, don't you?"

I was growing very impatient.

"No. I mean it's your home, your sister's home, home to all the Anabe. As it always has been."

Cole produced a document that he held out for all to see.

"This gives you legal title to Tawkenin. That's a beau-tiful name you know, Tawkenin. I always preferred it to Gold Medal Village. That's even too pretentious for my blood."

Cole smiled warmly, then reiterated.

"Congratulations Aupetchi. You won. Congratula-tions, and thank you."

Cole's generosity stunned me, initially. Finally I smiled and whooped with joy when I realized that Sawmay had been right all along. I had swum with the spirit of our ancestors and was strengthened by the depth of our faith. Anabe history would now tell of how I had been chosen to swim this race to fulfill this destiny. Tawkenin was saved.

The north and south villages would continue to buzz with activity. Our rich Anabe culture would continue to be embraced by our youth. Mishe Mokwa would continue to be our sacred water. I would continue to be Odawgen.

COLE

I could see that Kate was as stunned as Aupetchi. She had already accepted my marriage proposal, based upon the generosity of my original compromise and on my heroics during the storm. This act overwhelmed her. It was an extraordinary turn of events.

Aupetchi accepted the document and shook my hand again, this time with genuine sincerity. He now fully understood what had occurred. I would keep my word. Kate gave me a suffocating hug and May broke into appreciative tears. Olivia reached out and affectionately tousled my hair. Finally I broke away from Kate's clinch.

"There is one small technicality we have to take care of," I said. "To make it legal."

Suddenly Aupetchi and Maymegwan's faces mirrored distrust and disappointment. They seemed to expect the worst.

"I need to be compensated by you for the land," I continued, "in some form. I can't legally give you something for nothing and Tawkenin is mine in the eyes of the law. If you don't give me something, anything, someone will eventually get the courts to rule that our contract is void and you could lose the land. I don't want to see that happen, so you just have to give me something. A dollar even."

"I will not buy what is already mine. I can give you no money," Aupetchi replied.

"That's all right. I looked into this. It doesn't have to be money, just something of value. Like your sister's quillwork. I know that gets top dollar in Mackinaw City," Cole offered.

"But I have none, they have all been sold," May said.

"There must be something you have that you can give me!"

"A carving?" suggested Kate.

Aupetchi looked at her and smiled. She was right. That would be prefect.

"I have some of your carvings with me now," May-megwan volunteered. Kate had asked her to bring them.

"That would be fine," I said.

Maymegwan handed Aupetchi a small satchel. In it were six Petoskey stone carvings. Aupetchi instructed us to sit with him on the sand, in a circle. Then he reached into the sack and removed an image that he hid in his fist.

"Kate," he began, "we would not be here today without your help. Because I followed the trace from Tawkenin to this blissful shore we became friends. Now my people will live in their *wigwoms* forever and will continue to honor the land of our ancestors. This would not be true without you. You have generously given your kindness and your wisdom to my family, to my nation, and most of all, to me. I can never thank you enough."

Then he handed her the hidden fetish. She accepted it, gazed upon it and began to cry. She gave Aupetchi an affectionate hug. I smiled approvingly. After calming herself Kate attempted to explain her tears.

"It's a heron," she smiled, wiping a tear from her check, "made from the stone I found here, on Bliss Beach! Thank you."

Aupetchi returned her smile with a warm nod as Kate nestled comfortably into my arms, her future husband's arms. Then he reached into his bag once more.

"Cole," he said purposefully, "you have asked me to compensate you for the land of my people, the resting place of my grandparents and great-grandparents. I cannot do this."

At Kate and May's silent urging I accepted this news gracefully, without comment. Aupetchi continued.

"However, I must acknowledge the strength of your character," he added knowingly. "I recognize the purity in what you have said and done on this day. I wish to sanctify this fact. You may consider it compensation if you wish."

Aupetchi handed me the eloquent wolf carving, the same carving I had offered to buy at the Pow Wow. He continued to speak.

"Two weeks ago we raced together, as equals. I beat you only because I had the most to lose. One week ago we both battled the elements to save Kate. We struggled for the same purpose. You have shown me that some *waubesh* possess a pure heart. You have proven that a man's character can change, that destiny can be altered. Please accept this and know that I give it to you because I now see that you walk and swim with the spirit of the wolf."

"Thank you Aupetchi. I am humbled by your kindness," I replied honestly. Then I added, "And we now have a deal, a legal deal. This wolf fetish seals it."

As if on cue, we all turned in unison towards the lake, where the water lapped with soft sounds against the shore. The peal of a single creature broke the rhythm: A bird emerged from the mouth of a small river upshore. We attentively watched as it landed in the shallow water near us.

It was a blue heron. The creature held its body high above the surface, strutting on a pair of thin, stork-like legs. It arched its long, curved neck and peered directly at the mesmerized cluster of humanity. Each of us returned his stare.

"Manitou gives us a mysterious and beautiful world to live in," Aupetchi stated reverently.

"Amen," agreed Olivia.

Farther out on the lake a small sailboat glided below the slowly descending sun, temporarily hidden behind a single billowing cloud. Rays of purple, blue and orange radiated from behind the giant puff and reflected off the tranquil lake. All of us except Kate returned our gaze to the sunset. Out of the corner of my eye I noticed that she still held the bird's gaze. After a moment the blue heron seemed to wink at Kate. Then, as if to eliminate all doubt, it winked again.

"Thank you," she said, "for being there for me."

The heron held her gaze a few moments longer, then took flight and gracefully returned to the river.

Printed in the United States
32941LVS00012B/1

9 781932 560756